CW00847430

At Ardilla

Also by Gillian Rubinstein

Answers to Brut
Beyond the Labyrinth
Flashback
Melanie and the Night Animal
Skymaze
Space Demons

GILLIAN RUBINSTEIN

At Ardilla

MAMMOTH

First published in Australia by Omnibus Books,
Norwood, South Australia
First published in Great Britain 1991
by William Heinemann Ltd
Published 1993 by Mammoth
an imprint of Reed Consumer Books Ltd
Michelin House, 81 Fulham Road, London SW3 6RB
and Auckland, Melbourne, Singapore and Toronto

Reprinted 1993

Copyright © 1991 by Gillian Rubinstein

The right of Gillian Rubinstein to be identified as
the author of this work has been asserted by her in
accordance with the Copyright, Designs and Patents Act,
1988

ISBN 0 7497 0835 2

A CIP catalogue record for this title
is available from the British Library

Printed and bound in Great Britain
by Cox & Wyman Ltd, Reading, Berkshire

This paperback is sold subject to the condition
that it shall not, by way of trade or otherwise,
be lent, resold, hired out, or otherwise circulated
without the publisher's prior consent in any form
of binding or cover other than that in which
it is published and without a similar condition
including this condition being imposed
on the subsequent purchaser.

The author, in writing this book, was assisted by a Category A Fellowship from the Literary Arts Board of the Australia Council, the Federal Government's arts funding and advisory body.

This one is for the Hatt-Cooks

1

"Lisa, if you sing that song again, I'll kill you!"

Lisa Gilroy stopped singing, but only to appeal to her mother, in the front seat of the car. "I can sing if I want to, can't I, Mum?"

"You're not singing the right tune," Jen, her older sister, groaned. "It's driving me crazy."

"Driving you? You're crazy already." Lisa made a face at her sister and started singing again defiantly. Jen kicked her.

"Ouch!" Lisa's pretty face wrinkled up in pain and outrage. "Dad! Jen just kicked me."

"Girls!" Their father did not take his eyes off the road but his voice was sharp.

"Sit still!" Their mother turned round and gave them a stern look. "You'll make us have an accident." Then, remembering that they were on holiday and meant to be relaxing, she smiled and said placatingly, "Be patient. It's not long now. Why don't you sing something together? We'll all sing."

"You can't sing with Lisa," Jen said. "She's always in the wrong key!"

"I'm not!" Lisa exclaimed. "Just because you're the *muuuu*sical one! You think no one else can sing a note. I'm in the school orchestra too, you know! And I sang a solo in the Year Five choir."

"Don't remind me," Jen said. "All the bats in the hall died of shock and fell out of the roof. They were the only ones who could hear you, luckily for everyone else. You were singing beyond the pitch of the human ear."

If Lisa had said that to Jen, Jen would have sulked for the rest of the journey; but Lisa, who was good-natured and sunny, just laughed. "That's funny!" she said cheerfully. "Poor little bats, crashing down from the roof on everyone's head. Can't you just imagine it! Mr Jones would have a fit!"

"He'd be trying to hit them with his baton," Jen said, a smile lighting her serious, rather brooding face. "I'm so glad I'll never have to have orchestra with him any more!"

"You'll still be having orchestra," her mother put in swiftly. "You'll be in the high school orchestra."

"You never know," Jen said. "I might not be good enough!"

The whole family laughed at that. Jen was joking, of course. There was no question of her not being good enough. Music was something that came effortlessly to her. All her life people had been telling first her parents, and lately herself, that she appeared to have real talent. Her mother, a music teacher and ambitious for her, never allowed her to forget it.

"Anyway," Jen went on, "that's not till next term. We've got weeks of lovely holidays till then. No getting up early, no rushing around, no sport, no music."

"Yes music," Mrs Gilroy put in firmly. "You still have to practise. You did remember to put your flute in, didn't you?"

"Yes, Mum! Thank God the piano's too big to put in the car! I'm surprised they didn't strap it on the roof," she said in an undertone to Lisa.

Thinking about leaving the routine of school behind and escaping to Ardilla, where strict everyday rules were laid aside and even parents relaxed, reminded her of something else.

"Do you realise I don't go to school any more?" she said, giving Lisa a friendly but superior nudge with her elbow.

"You do so!" Lisa replied.

"No I don't," Jen said, running her hands through her black, spiky hair and grinning. "I've left primary school and I'm not at high school yet. So I don't go to school any more! *Wooo!* And you do!" she added, just in case Lisa had not got the point.

"Let's sing something," Mrs Gilroy said again, hastily.

"It's too hot," Jen said. She stared out of the window at the summer landscape baking in the late afternoon sun. Wheatfields, recently harvested, stretched away to the distant shimmer of the sea. On her left lay round purple hills.

Lisa wriggled impatiently. "How much longer is it, Dad?"

Jen hardly listened to her father's reply. She knew exactly where she was, and how much longer the journey would take. She had been making it once, sometimes twice a year, for ten years, since she was two. She knew exactly how far she was from Ardilla. She could feel it getting closer and closer. Closing her eyes, she could see it clearly, standing at the end of the long, pine-shaded driveway, waiting for her.

The Gilroys spent part of every summer at Ardilla with their friends the Melvilles. Jen was passionate about the place. It meant more to her than anywhere else in the

3

world. Each time she saw it she took possession of it. Or did it take possession of her? She conveniently forgot the other people who rented Ardilla at other times of the year. The old house and tumbledown outbuildings, the stone-walled paddocks, the tea-trees on the dunes, the little beach, the rocks and the island, these all belonged to her, to be shared of course with Lisa and their friends Tom and Richy Melville, and to a lesser extent with the parents of the two families—but not with anyone else!

Through the car window she glimpsed a familiar tree, one side blackened by fire. Two cows stood beneath it.

"Hello," she said silently to the tree. In less than an hour they would be there. Usually at this stage of the journey she was jumping with excitement, but this year she felt only apprehension. She couldn't forget that for the first time there were going to be strangers at Ardilla.

Mrs Gilroy and Lisa were singing quietly, Lisa taking the melody and her mother the harmony, but after two or three songs they fell silent. Mrs Gilroy's eyes closed. Lisa sneaked a look at her and then leaned over to Jen and whispered in her ear, "Bird overheard!"

"Sssh," Jen said, making a gesture towards the adults in the front seat. Lisa had spoken the first line of a secret chant, known only to her and Jen, and to Tom and Richy Melville.

"They can't hear," Lisa mouthed, her blue eyes bright with excitement. "I can't wait to do the Club again with Tom and Richy. Do you reckon all the things are still there?"

Jen had a clear picture of the packet, wrapped in the slithery black material Richy swore was sharkskin, stowed away at the end of last year's holiday, under the slate roof at Ardilla. It contained all the secrets of

4

the Club, put together over the years—the treasures found on the beach: crab claw, black feather, bird's skull and fish skeleton, each one with its own history and meaning, chants and codes, made up by Tom Melville and written out in dark red Texta like blood, along with other symbols and signs, powerful and private.

In other years this picture would have added to her excitement. This year it simply increased her tension.

"Do you think everyone will still want to do the Club?" she muttered.

"Of course they will!" Lisa was so shocked she forgot to whisper. "We can't not do the Club at Ardilla."

"That other family's going to be there," Jen said, wanting to share her apprehension with her sister. "The ones Dad asked," she added, raising her voice so her father could hear her clearly.

"Aww!" Lisa groaned. "I'd forgotten them! Dad, why did you have to ask them? They're going to spoil everything."

"You might wait till you get to know them before you decide you don't like them," Mr Gilroy replied, defensively. "Joe Fraser seems to be quite a nice man, lots of fun."

"What does that mean, 'lots of fun'?" Lisa said suspiciously. "I suppose he makes weak jokes all the time."

"We're not going to like them," Jen said. "We didn't want them to come. It was all your brilliant idea."

"I felt sorry for Joe," her father explained. "His wife took off to Melbourne last year and took all the kids with her. Now he's got them for the holidays, but he lives in a unit in the city. I reckoned it made good sense to ask them to share Ardilla with us." He sounded a little doubtful about it, and added, "I hope it all works out!"

Mrs Gilroy opened her eyes and said, "I must say, it's not like you to be so friendly to people! I was quite surprised when you told me you'd invited them. But I think it's a very good idea. We've always thought we should try and find another family. The house is big enough."

"And expensive enough," Mr Gilroy added.

"All you ever think about is money!" Jen said bitterly.

"And all you ever think about is yourself!" he replied swiftly, anger building up in his voice.

"Come on," Lisa pleaded. "We said we weren't going to have any rows on holiday."

"I don't start the rows," Jen said. "Everyone else is always fighting with me! Mum's always running my life, and Dad's always bossing me around!"

She scowled at the back of her father's neck. She could see his face in the rearvision mirror, scowling too, so like hers that for a moment she thought it was her own.

"I expect you to be friendly to the Frasers," he said warningly. There was an extra line of tension between his eyes, a deep groove.

"Dad!" Jen said. "Lighten up a bit. We're on holiday."

He did not answer, but rubbed his eyes with one hand.

"Do you want me to drive?" Mrs Gilroy asked. "You're not getting a headache, are you?"

"No," he said loudly. "I am not getting a headache."

"You'd better not," Jen said in alarm. "It'll ruin things even more if you get migraine at Ardilla!"

"It may be news to you, but I don't actually choose to get migraine," her father said sarcastically.

Jen always had to have the last word. "People do choose to be ill," she said. "And you're so uptight, that's why you get migraine!"

"Jennifer, that's enough," her mother said sharply.

"It's not my fault you're both uptight. You're the ones that make us all so busy." Jen was thinking resentfully of her crammed days: early morning practice, the dash to sports after school, practice again at night.

"Life's too short to waste," her mother said. As if to illustrate her point she took out an emery board and began filing her nails. "If you want to make anything of yourself you've got to work for it. And now's the time you've got to learn good habits—you're very talented at music, but it's going to take a lot of work and a lot of practising to get there. Next year's going to be harder for you—high school is very different from primary school. You won't be able to mooch around any more."

Jen looked stormier than ever. She'd heard this particular speech many times before. But she said nothing.

"Thank goodness we've got a few weeks to mooch around at Ardilla then," Lisa said, trying to cheer everyone up.

But the Frasers are going to be at Ardilla too, Jen thought, gazing out of the window and realising they were nearly there. And what's Ardilla going to be like with strangers in it? She sighed heavily, feeling depression creep over her.

Even the sight of Ardilla at the end of the driveway could not quite lift her black mood. The old stone homestead stood before them, honey coloured in the evening sun, splashed with purple bougainvillaea, surrounded by white and yellow cape daisies. Seen from the shade of the old pine trees that lined the driveway, the house still looked like a magic place, and Jen felt the same familiar rush of love for it, but she could not get rid of the feeling that something threatened the magic.

"Every year I'm surprised it's still standing," Mr Gilroy said, as the car came to a halt.

"It could certainly do with some work," his wife agreed.

Jen saw for a moment two Ardillas—the same old magic one, perfect and beautiful, and the Ardilla of this particular year, showing signs of wear, shabbier, more faded, with new cracks in the stonework. Then the two merged and she could no longer tell one from the other.

Mr Gilroy opened his door with a sigh. "Everybody take something in!" he ordered, but in vain. Jen and Lisa had already jumped from the car and were running towards the house.

Pigeons cooed peacefully from the roof. The air smelt of salt and seaweed and rosemary. The old building seemed to stretch in the sun like a purring cat.

The two girls padded, barefoot, over the wooden veranda.

"Jen, Lisa!" their father shouted.

"OK, OK!" Jen called back. The boards beneath her feet were still warm from the sun. She was noticing as she spoke their smooth silvery look, remembering with her toes the exact feel of them. She added quietly, sure he could not hear her, "We just have to do the Look."

They stood without speaking, lightly holding the rail of the veranda. Behind them the silent house waited, full of secrets. In front of them the paddock, faded grass cropped short by sheep, sloped away to the dunes and the bay. The sea was dark evening blue and dead flat, showing only a fraction of lacy white round the rocky island. The sky was streaked with pale grey clouds that were just beginning to turn pink.

"Look," Jen breathed quietly. Her eyes swept across the bay, reclaiming it.

"I look!" Lisa replied, dramatically. She threw her hands up in the air, and as if in response a black cormorant rose from the distant rocks of the island and flew heavily across the bay.

Jen followed its flight with narrowed, greenish eyes. Was the cormorant, almost the first thing they had seen in the Look, welcoming her, signalling to her? She said nothing, but she bit her knuckles hard. Already they tasted faintly salty.

"Oh, lucky!" Lisa said, but without real envy, for in this as in everything she recognised that Jen had a special claim to Ardilla. Lisa loved the place too, loved being there, but she did not feel the same aching longing that Jen had to possess every part of Ardilla and keep it for herself alone.

"I wish the Melvilles'd hurry up," Lisa said, turning away. For her the Look was over and finished with. She wanted to get on with the more practical part of the holidays, like getting down to the beach as soon as possible with Richy and Tom.

"Oh, wait a minute!" Jen wanted to linger for a few moments, to squeeze the last drop of feeling out of the magical evening light. Her mother often told her that was the trouble with her—she tried to squeeze life dry, take too much from it. From people too, as if she could not be happy with just ordinary surface friendships. She wanted everything from everybody. It made her intense and jealous, passionate and moody.

Now she scowled after her sister as Lisa darted back to the car. Then the beauty of the scene before her drew her eyes back to the bay. The cormorant was perched on the rocks again, making a mournful cry, as if calling to its mate. Jen ignored her parents' demands for help. Rapt, she gazed out to sea, listening to secret voices in her head.

First comes the Look.

Our eyes receive this place back again. It's still here. It's survived another year. We see it all and we own it all. For another year it's ours again. What was the cormorant saying to me? Was it an accident it flew up when it did, or was it giving me some message? Was it perhaps saying it's up to me to keep this place safe? The cormorant is special to me, as the crab is to Richy, the fish to Tom, and the sandpiper to Lisa. We chose these things, or they chose us, so long ago we've forgotten why. They are our totems. We look after them and they look after us. They are the creatures that keep everything safe at Ardilla. When I'm away they look after it. And now I'm back and the cormorant knows it. It saw me and it flew across the bay, giving Ardilla back to me.

Bird overheard,
Crab, grab,
Fish, wish,
Birds words.
At Ardilla, at Ardilla, at Ardilla!
These are words made up by kids, but they have power.

2

The sun was almost setting, a huge orange ball colouring the whole scene with an unnatural hallucinatory glow. The wind blew a little more strongly round the eaves of the house, making Jen shiver in her thin T-shirt.

I must get a jumper, she thought, and was turning to leave the veranda when she heard the noise of a car coming up the drive. Lisa, who was unloading gear from their own car, shouted with excitement.

"They're coming, they're coming!"

Jen ran down the steps. Lisa was already at the end of the driveway, dancing up and down and brandishing a snorkel. It was dark under the pine trees and the approaching car had its headlights on so that the girls could not see it clearly until it was very close. They fell back sheepishly. Lisa tried to hide the snorkel behind her back. It was not Tom and Richy and their parents. It was the other family, the Frasers.

Even their car looked completely out of place. An avocado-green Mercedes, it was too new and flashy against the old, weathered buildings. As the sun set Ardilla turned grey and unwelcoming. It doesn't like them, Jen thought with satisfaction. And nor do I!

With a strange feeling of relief, she watched them get out of the car. She knew instantly she was right not to like them.

11

There were three children, two boys and a girl. The girl was the oldest. She was wearing stonewash jeans and white leather sneakers. Her socks and her T-shirt were exactly the same shade of red and she wore red clips in her hair. A navy-blue windcheater was knotted over her shoulders. She was slim and sun-tanned and she looked about eighteen.

A spooner, Jen thought savagely. A posing spooner.

The older boy was also smartly dressed and his hair was cut in a trendy style. He was pale and his face had a shuttered look to it. Jen decided instantly he was sly.

It was impossible to tell anything about the little boy. He clung hard to his sister's hand and did not want to go to anyone else.

"Jen!" her father called. "Come and say hello!"

Mr Fraser was a large man, tall and overweight, and the heat of the drive had made him sweat. He held out a huge meaty hand to Jen and she took it reluctantly.

"G'day, love," he said, too friendly for her liking. "You're the child prodigy, are you? The infant James Galway, hey?"

"Not exactly," Jen said, swearing inwardly at her father. How dare he brag about her to strangers! Mr Fraser did not listen to her reply.

"And this is your gorgeous sister! Wow! Another couple of years and you'll be breaking a few hearts, won't you, sweetheart?"

Jen's mother flinched a bit at this. "I'm sure she'll be much too sensible," she said, with a laugh.

"Don't you believe it, Di! Look at my Sally. Last year she was a tomboy. This year she's boy mad."

"Daaad!" Sally exclaimed.

"Let's go in," Mr Gilroy said, changing the subject,

Jen noticed. She knew her parents still thought of her and Lisa as just kids, nowhere near teenage. Mr Fraser's talk was disturbing her father. You can't stop us growing up, Dad, she told him inside her head, wishing she could talk to him more easily about this and so many other things.

"I expect you could use a drink," Mr Gilroy offered awkwardly.

"Never spoke a truer word, mate. It won't even touch the sides!"

"Hello, Sally," Mrs Gilroy said. "These are our daughters, Jen, and Lisa. Jen's about the same age as you, I think. She's twelve."

"I turned thirteen in October," Sally said. She started to smile at Jen, but Jen's cold face stopped her.

"And you must be Mark?" Mrs Gilroy went on, sounding more and more determinedly friendly in the face of Jen and Lisa's hostility.

The boy nodded, but said nothing.

"And this is our little brother, Nicky!" Sally said brightly.

"Hello, Nicky dear! Jen, Lisa, say hello to Nicky!"

Nicky did not want to say hello to anyone. He put his thumb in his mouth and tried to hide behind Sally.

"Bring your bags in, dear," Mrs Gilroy said to Sally, "and I'll show you where you and your brothers are going to sleep."

"Go with Daddy," Sally said to the little boy, who had transferred his grip from her hand to the back of her jeans, leaving a smear of chocolate just behind the knee.

He looked doubtfully after the adults and clung harder.

"Go on, Nicky," she said. "Sal's got to carry the bags in."

13

"Jen and Lisa can take them," Mrs Gilroy said firmly, giving Jen a push.

"Here," Lisa said, taking Sally's tote bag from her hand, "give me this."

Scowling terribly, Jen picked up a suitcase. "You brought an awful lot of stuff," she grumbled. "You probably won't need half of it."

Sally gave her a sharp look. Then she tilted her head back and spoke to Jen's mother. "What a great place this is! It was kind of you to ask us. I bet we'll have a fantastic time!"

"Suck!" Jen muttered to herself as she lugged the smart new suitcase inside and up the narrow stairs that led to the two attic bedrooms.

This was where the children always slept when they came to Ardilla. It was their private territory, where adults usually never intruded. The two bedrooms were separated by a small landing known as Neutral Ground. Jen and Lisa slept on one side, Tom and Richy on the other.

Going into the room that should have been hers and Lisa's, Jen dropped the suitcase with a thunk on the splintery floorboards.

"Be careful with that, Jen," her mother said automatically. "Sally, you'd better take one of the beds, you're a bit taller than our girls. Which one would you like?"

"Oh, the one under the window will be fine," Sally said smoothly, looking round the little room with its whitewashed walls and curious dormer window that gave out on to the roof.

"But it's my turn for the window bed," Lisa exclaimed in outrage. "Jen had it last year, and I've been looking forward to it all year."

"Do be sensible, Lisa!" Mrs Gilroy sounded angry. "You're the shortest, so you'll have to sleep on the stretcher."

"It's not fair," Lisa groaned. "Why can't she sleep on the stretcher?"

"Lisa," her mother said sharply. "Sally is our visitor."

Sally pointedly took no part in this argument. She simply set about unpacking her things and putting them in the tiny cupboard and on the chest. Since she had such a lot of stuff it soon looked as though she had taken over the room.

"Good!" Mrs Gilroy said to no one in particular, while Jen and Lisa smouldered silently. "Now you, Mark." She led him across Neutral Ground and into the other bedroom. "You can go in here with Tom and Richy. You'll get on well with them, they're very nice boys. You're quite tall too, aren't you? You'd better have the bed and we'll bring up an air mattress for Richy. Come and give me a hand, Jen."

Jen followed her mother down the stairs, scowling more than ever.

"Try and be nice to them!" her mother hissed when they were out of earshot.

"Why should I? I didn't ask them to come." Jen spoke in her normal voice and then noticed Mr Fraser standing inside the downstairs bedroom that was going to be his and Nicky's. He was unfolding his clothes and whistling slightly off key. He gave her a wink through the half-open door.

He heard me, she thought. Well, I don't care. He might as well know I don't want him and his horrible kids around, and I am not going to try and be nice to them.

15

"Don't be rude!" Mrs Gilroy whispered. She had seen the wink too.

She wants me to be polite so I'm not letting her down, Jen grumbled inwardly. Just wants me to make a good impression. Not only brilliantly talented but nice and polite too! She and Dad always want things to look right even if they're all wrong underneath. It's not fair! If I can't be myself at Ardilla, where can I be!

Jen felt a rush of irritation. She wanted to strip the protective cover off the surface of her life. She wanted everyone to be truthful, even if it was painful. But she knew there was no point saying any of these things to her mother. It would only provoke another lecture. So she dutifully unloaded the air mattress from the boot of their car and took it up to the boys' bedroom, where Mark was carefully stowing something away under the bed.

"Here you are," she said, chucking the mattress at him. "You can start blowing it up, since you pinched Richy's bed. And he's going to get you for that," she added meanly. "You won't have a peaceful night's sleep the whole time you're here."

Mark's impassive face did not change, nor did he pick up the air mattress.

Jen looked at the long green canvas bag Mark had put away under the bed. "What's that?" she said suspiciously.

"Don't touch it," Mark warned.

"What's in it?"

"It's my fishing gear."

"Fishing gear? You're not going to go fishing here!"

"Why not?"

"We don't go fishing here," Jen replied, her heart jumping with anger.

"Well, I'm going to."

16

CU00847430

At Ardilla

"You won't be allowed to!"

Mark turned away from Jen and looked out of the window. Then he opened the sash and stuck his head out.

"Sally!" he called. "Look out the window!"

Sally opened the window in the girls' room and stuck her head out too. "Neat! You could climb out on to the roof."

"You aren't allowed on the roof either!" Jen said hastily.

"Strictly forbidden," Lisa agreed. They exchanged horrified looks across Neutral Ground. Of all the special places at Ardilla, this was the most special. Over the slope of the roof, in the valley between the two gables, was the place where the four children held the Club.

Both the Club and the place they held it in were typical of all the magical things that happened at Ardilla. At home none of them was ever allowed to do anything the least bit risky—Saturday morning sport was about their most dangerous activity. Both the Gilroy and the Melville parents were strict and rather over-protective, but when they came to Ardilla something happened to them. It was as though they put off being responsible adults for a while. They took a break from always making sure that their children were growing up in the right way, brushing their teeth night and morning, getting nine hours' sleep at night, developing habits of self-discipline and not running any risks. Everybody relaxed at Ardilla. The parents read a lot of novels, drank more in the evenings than they normally did, lay on the sand and did nothing for hours on end. They left the children to their own devices. After all, they reasoned, what could possibly go wrong at Ardilla? There were a few rules— not going out in the dinghy without a lifejacket was one—but the little bay was quite safe for swimming, and the children were able to run wild in a way they never did in the city.

Mostly they did nothing really dangerous, although they had had a few narrow escapes that their parents knew nothing about. And they climbed over the roof to hold the meetings of the Club.

Now, here were the strangers, Sally and Mark, threatening to invade their most precious territory.

"Sounds like there's an awful lot of things you aren't allowed to do in this place," Mark said scornfully. "Our dad doesn't mind what we do. He'll take me fishing, and he'll let me go on the roof!"

Before Jen could answer this, a little voice sang out from the top of the stairs. "Sally!"

"Nicky," she replied, and ran over to pick him up.

"I climbed the stairs!"

"You're a clever boy!"

Jen groaned and Lisa rolled her eyes back in her head.

Sally staggered across the room with Nicky, pretending he was really heavy. "Look out the window, Nicky! See the little island. Isn't it gorgeous!"

Nicky held on to the windowsill with exaggerated caution. "Car coming!" he exclaimed.

"It's the Melvilles," Lisa said.

Jen thought dully how happy they would normally be, how they would be hanging out of the window and waving and shouting to Tom and Richy. Instead, this year, they were standing around awkwardly with three children they hated. It's all spoiled, she said bitterly to herself. Ardilla is wrecked.

3

Nicky climbed carefully down from the window, stepped backwards and fell over the air mattress.

"What's this, Sally?" he said, trying to pick it up.

"It's an air mattress. You blow it up; one of the boys is going to sleep on it."

"Blow!" Nicky commanded, holding out the air mattress to Mark. Then he changed his mind and with an eager smile said, "Nicky blow!" He put his mouth to it and blew till his face turned red and his eyes started to pop. Then he looked at the flat mattress.

"Not getting big!" he said, disappointed.

Mark smiled. "You can't blow it up, Nicky. You're too little! Here, give it to me."

He took the mattress and blew ferociously into it. Little by little it began to swell. He was still puffing away when there was a clatter of feet on the attic stairs and the two Melville boys appeared on Neutral Ground.

They could have been twins, almost the same height, with similar sun-bleached hair and brown eyes.

"You're up here!" the younger one, Richy, exclaimed. "You didn't come out to meet us!" Then he looked around, noticed Jen and Lisa's stony faces and said, "What's up?"

"These kids are what's up," Jen replied. "Up here."

"Hi," Richy said in his usual friendly way, looking

from Sally to Nicky to Mark, who gave one final huge puff into the air mattress. He smiled as he handed it to Richy. "Here you are, I blew it up for you."

It sagged limply between them. Richy looked at it dubiously. "Am I sleeping on this?"

"Their mum said," Mark said, and sat down on one of the beds.

"Oh."

There was a moment's awkward silence. Eventually Lisa said grudgingly, "This is Sally, and Mark, and the little one is Nicky."

"They're staying here for the whole three weeks," Jen added.

"Oh, great!" Richy said, naturally polite. "I'm Richard Melville and this is my brother, Tom."

Tom had been stricken by total shyness and was unloading his things on the other bed. He said hello in the general direction of his pillow as he unpacked a snorkel and face mask, a pair of binoculars, his camera and two books on marine life. He put these carefully on the bedside table, left his clothes in his bag, and shoved it under the bed.

"Hi!" Sally said brightly. "Nice camera!"

Tom sneaked a quick glance at her and smiled.

He's smiling at her, Jen thought in horror. He can't be going to like her! He's much too sensible for that! Tom was Jen's oldest friend—they had practically grown up together ever since their mothers had met in hospital when they were born. Tom was clever and resourceful. He knew all about the wildlife of the beach and dunes. He could construct weird machines from the junk in the outbuildings. He made up the chants and codes for the Club. There was no way she was going to let Tom be friends with Sally Fraser, the spooner.

Richy chucked the air mattress down on the floor and dropped his bag on top of it.

"How old are you?" he asked Mark when no one else spoke.

"Ten," Mark replied proudly.

"So'm I! How about that!" Richy grinned as if he was really pleased at this amazing coincidence. "You want to come and have a look round? Bring your bathers—we can have a swim." Then he noticed the icy atmosphere in the room and said to Lisa, "What's wrong with everyone?"

"You're being a traitor, that's what's wrong," Jen said angrily.

Richy looked at her, his smile fading. Then he said, trying to whisper, "What's wrong with them? Don't you like them?"

Sally's chin went up and she said coolly, "I'm not staying here to be talked about. Come on, Nicky, let's go and find Daddy. Then we'll fix you up with some tea!"

They heard her voice from the bottom of the stairs. "Can I give you a hand with that, Mrs Gilroy?"

"Thank you, dear! I hope you're settling in all right. Are the girls being nice to you?"

"Sure," Sally answered. "Just wait there, Nicky, I'll be down in a sec."

They struggled up the stairs with the stretcher bed. If Mrs Gilroy noticed the tension in the room she did not mention it. When she and Sally had gone again, Richy said, "Let's go and swim!"

The adults were downstairs in the kitchen, putting away the food they had brought and talking up a storm.

"John's brought half the wine cellar with him," Mrs Melville said with a laugh to Mrs Gilroy.

"Plenty of white for you, Tony!" said Mr Melville. "I know the reds are fatal for your head!"

"I'll probably stick with beer," Mr Gilroy said from the fridge, where he was trying to find room for all the bottles.

"Oh, but this is something really special I got in Victoria last year!"

"What do you want to go to Victoria for when you've got the best wines in the world on your doorstep!" Mr Fraser asked. He was standing by the sink, a bottle of beer in his hand.

"Did you bring plenty of books?" Mrs Gilroy said to Mrs Melville. "I'm just going to read and read all holidays."

"I've got a novel you'll love! I've almost finished it." Mrs Melville skirted her way round Mr Fraser. "Excuse me, Joe, I just want to put this under the sink."

"She was reading all the way in the car," Richy said. "I don't know how you can, Mum, it makes me feel sick."

"Got into practice on the school bus! Forty minutes each way every day. I read my way through the entire library."

"Where did you grow up?" Mr Fraser asked. "Back of Bourke somewhere?"

"Not quite—mid-north area. I went to Gladstone High."

"Country girl," Mr Fraser said. "We'll expect you to hew the wood and fetch the water out here in the outback!"

Mrs Melville gave him a sardonic look. "This is a liberated household, mate. Everyone hews their own wood!"

"Ardilla's hardly the outback," Lisa said, taking the lid off the plastic container Mrs Melville had just put on the table, and helping herself to a biscuit. "It's only a few minutes' drive to Frewin Bay."

"It feels like a million miles from anywhere, though. Lisa, darling, take just one of those bikkies and then put them in the pantry."

"Come on, let's go and swim," Richy said urgently. "You can do the unpacking, can't you, Mum?"

"There speaks one unliberated male," Mr Fraser joked. "Why don't I go down to the beach with all the kids? I'm only in the way here."

"You're certainly big enough to be in the way," Mrs Melville said, tapping him on the chest. "We'd better put you to work! Sweat off some of that excess weight!"

"I'm going to get into shape while I'm here," Mr Fraser said, laughing.

"You won't have a chance," Mrs Gilroy said. "Not with John's cooking."

"Bit of a gourmet chef, eh?"

Mr Melville made a bow, flourishing a tea-towel in the air. "That's part of the fun of the holiday for me. I do the evening meals and Tony does the lunches."

"What do you women do, then?" Mr Fraser said, pretending to be outraged.

"We lie around and read books!" Mrs Gilroy said with a giggle.

"And work on our sun-tans," Mrs Melville added. "That's very important!"

"Can we please go down to the beach, Dad?" Mark pulled at his father's sleeve.

"For sure!" Mr Fraser downed the remains of his beer at a gulp. "Can't wait to get in the water myself. Who else is coming?"

In a few minutes they had sorted out who was going and who was staying. Jen was in the laundry collecting the surf mats when she heard her mother talking to Sally.

"Don't you want to go too?"

"No, I don't want to take Nicky down now. He'll get too wet before bedtime and I'm afraid he'll get cold."

"You're a very responsible big sister! You must be a great help to your mother!"

"Mum's gone back to work now," Sally replied. "I babysit Nicky every day after school."

"Well, you can leave him with me and run down to the beach with the others!" Mrs Gilroy suggested.

Oops, I'm out of here! Jen thought, and left the laundry as quietly as she could. Climbing over the paddock wall she dropped one of the mats, and as she bent to pick it up a movement up near the house caught her eye.

A little figure in red shorts was running over the grass. Closer to the kitchen door someone was standing watching him. It was Sally.

She stood slightly slumped, her weight on one leg, as though she was deathly tired. Her arms were crossed over her chest, her hands gripping her shoulders. She looked far, far older than a thirteen-year-old girl, and she looked sad with a private sadness that Jen felt excluded from and offended by.

She didn't want to feel sorry for Sally. She wanted to feel angry with her. The anger made her feel strong and alive. She was right to feel it. Sally was an intruder at Ardilla. The house and its guardians didn't want her there. Fuelled by it, she ran and jumped all the way down to the beach.

It was nearly dark. She could just make out two figures splashing each other in the water—Mark and his father. Her own father and Mrs Melville were standing on the water's edge, deep in conversation. Further up, near the dunes, Jen could see a dark huddle which, as she approached it, turned out to be Tom, Richy and Lisa. Jen dropped the surf mats in a pile and ran over to them.

They turned as they saw her, each holding out both hands with the little fingers crooked. The four of them linked fingers in a circle and began to sway backwards and forwards as they chanted,

All are id,
All are id,
Bird, fish,
Be witnesses,
Cormorant, crab,
We are back,
Sea, sand,
House, land,
All are ours,
All are id,
At Ardilla, at Ardilla, at Ardilla.

Jen swayed back and forwards as they repeated the chant, losing herself in the familiar hypnotic words, but before the end of the second time round there was a giggle. Tom backed out of the circle, dropping his hands abruptly and breaking away from the others as if he was angry.

"What's the matter?" Richy said.

"Nothing's the matter with me," Tom replied. "You're the one that was giggling."

"Sorry," Richy said, giggling again. "It just suddenly seemed really funny. And I kept thinking, what if Mark was watching us. He'd think we were mental!"

"Don't laugh," Lisa said. "It spoils it."

"We'll have to start again," Jen added. "And do the whole thing properly." She said quietly to Tom, "Were you saying it, anyway? I could hardly hear you!"

"Yeah, I was saying it," Tom answered, but his voice was awkward and he sounded embarrassed. He kept looking towards the water, where Mark was now diving off his father's shoulders. They could just make out the dark shapes and the splashes of white.

"They can't see us," Jen said. "Come on, let's finish the chanting and the dance. Lisa, do the sandpiper dance."

Tom laughed self-consciously. "I'm going to swim before it gets too dark. We'll finish it later, OK?"

"Tom," she said, feeling the anger still burning inside, "we've got to finish it once we've started."

Her father turned from the water's edge and called out to them, "Better swim if you're going to." Mrs Melville was already in the water. Jen could see her swimming near Mr Fraser and Mark. They splashed her as she went past and she turned and splashed them back.

"Come on," Richy said, wanting to join in the fun.

"You see," Jen said to Lisa as the two boys tore down to the water. "That's what I was afraid of. They don't want to do the Club with the Frasers here. Tom's embarrassed."

"We can do it later," Lisa replied. "There'll be plenty of time. Let's go. That water fight looks like fun!"

Mr Fraser threw himself into the fight with great seriousness and was as tireless as the children. He teased the three boys and Lisa and ducked them mercilessly when he could catch them. Jen retreated out of his way—

she didn't like to admit it, but she found him too rough.

On the way back to the house the others continued the rough-housing, jumping on the adults and trying to trip them up, while Jen trailed behind, alone, carrying the surf mats which in the end no one had used.

That turned out to be the pattern of the evening until bedtime and she didn't like it at all. She felt as if Tom, who had been like her twin brother for the last twelve years, was avoiding her. Still seeming self-conscious and shy, he was sticking close to Richy, who was happy to be the centre of the group, equally friendly to his old mate, Lisa, and his new one, Mark. The adults kept trying to push Jen and Sally together—"Jen, can you and Sally give us a hand with the washing up?" "Jen, why don't you and Sally have a game of cards?" "Jen, isn't it nice to have someone your own age here?"—until she had actually said in self-defence, "I think I'd better do some flute practice," and had taken herself out on the veranda to play, unable to believe that she was spending her first night at Ardilla practising without being told to.

When she came back inside again, Mr Fraser had organised a noisy game of Racing Demon and all the children were playing, except Nicky, who Sally had already put to bed in the room he was sharing with his father.

"You are a dedicated little thing, aren't you," Mr Fraser commented to Jen, not taking his eyes off the piles of cards as he slapped down a King.

Sally glanced up. "You don't fool me," her look said to Jen. "You think I don't know why you suddenly had to go and play the flute?" She smiled slightly to herself, moved three cards amazingly rapidly and said, "Out!"

There was a groan of protest.

"You should be handicapped," Richy said in disgust. "You're too fast!"

"Just incredibly gifted at Racing Demon," Sally said. There was no trace of the tiredness or the sadness that had marked her before. She didn't look self-conscious or shy either. She looked very pleased with herself and disgustingly pretty.

"Jen usually wins when we play," Lisa said loyally.

"Why doesn't Jen play now?" Mr Fraser suggested, and when she refused, saying she didn't feel like it, he gave her another of his disturbing half-winks as he began to sort out the cards.

The three girls did not talk much when they went to bed. Lisa complained about having to sleep on the stretcher bed and how she felt as if she was suffocating down near the floor. Sally seemed to go to sleep quickly and quietly. For a while Jen listened to Richy and Mark chattering away on the other side of Neutral Ground, with the occasional remark from Tom. Then the boys fell silent. Lisa was snoring very gently. Everyone was asleep except her.

Jen was never a good sleeper and spent many nights restless and wakeful, but normally she slept better at Ardilla than at home. This night she tossed from side to side as the events of the day replayed themselves in her head.

The cormorant's flight and the unfinished rituals seemed linked with the Frasers' presence at Ardilla. They had already interfered with the Club. They were going to spoil everything. It was bad enough having the kids around all the time, but their father was worse. The way he looked at her as though he knew exactly what she was thinking. The way he teased everyone. His horrible winks and jokes.

I've already got someone my own age, she muttered to herself as she flipped over on to her other side. I like hanging around with Tom. And I know Sally's going to spoil it. When she did sleep it was only restlessly, and she was disturbed towards morning by curious vivid dreams that she could not quite remember when she woke.

*I always knew there were two Ardillas. There is the real
Ardilla that feels the winds in winter and the baking
summer sun. This Ardilla ages every year and will one
day crumble and fall down and be there no more. There
is the other Ardilla that exists magically in my memory,
always perfect and eternal. But now I know there is
another Ardilla, lying between the two, both beneath and
within them. Only I have entered it, walking with fear and
awe into rooms I did not know existed, amazed by their
beauty and their power.*

*I can go into it because I have been loyal to the
Guardians, the ancient ones that keep this place together.
I have fed them with the rituals they need and love. I keep
them alive and give them power, and in return they guard
this magic place and nourish me. But they are not safe.
They are not tame. To walk among them is to walk into
danger. It is better to leave them alone altogether than to
waken them and then abandon them.*

*If they are abandoned, if they are harmed, they
demand payment. They demand retribution.*

It was late in the morning when Jen woke and came
downstairs. The house was silent and deserted, but she
found her mother on the cane lounge on the veranda,
reading a book, a half-drunk cup of coffee next to her.

"Where is everyone, Mum?"

Mrs Gilroy finished her page before replying.

"They've all gone down to swim." She turned the page and then lifted her eyes to her daughter's face. "What happened to you? You must be turning into a teenager, lying in bed till nearly lunchtime!"

"I didn't sleep very well," Jen said, wanting her mother to ask why, so she could try to exorcise with words some of the crazy images that were still floating around in her head. A huge black bird, strange rooms that she had not known existed, being able to see with X-ray eyes, skeletons beneath the flesh.

Mrs Gilroy had gone back to her book.

"Uh-huh," she commented, without really listening.

Jen stood for a few seconds, feeling the cool air of the shaded veranda on her bare arms, and noticing the deep blue of the sea. She could see someone swimming right out in the middle of the bay.

"I might as well go and have a swim too."

"Good idea!" her mother agreed. "I'll come down later. Help yourself to something to eat before you go."

After the bright sunlight, the house inside was dark. Jen could hardly see as she made her way through to the kitchen. As she opened the door of the fridge to get a drink of milk, she had a strong sense that everything had happened exactly this way before. She shut the fridge door and spun round, almost expecting to see someone behind her, but the room was empty. She knew all about *déjà vu*, knew that it was a phenomenon of perception, but the experience had been so strong it made her shiver.

Something's going wrong, she thought. The milk was warmish and it tasted strange, not quite as milk should. She poured it down the sink and took a banana from the box in the pantry. The bunches of bananas looked weird too, like dead yellow hands that had started to rot. When

31

she bit into the banana she found she could not swallow. The fruit turned to cottonwool in her mouth. She ran outside and spat it into the daisies. Immediately ants started to crawl over it.

The sun was hot, but Jen was freezing. I don't feel well, she thought. I must be sick. I must be getting the flu. She went back to the veranda to talk to her mother again, but Mrs Gilroy was completely absorbed in her book.

Something had happened to Jen's perception. The veranda sloped away, distorted. The cane lounge clung to it like a leaf caught in a cobweb. Through Mrs Gilroy's solid body, Jen could see her bones; beneath the blonde hair, so like Lisa's, a fragile bird-like skull.

She caught her breath, feeling that if she were to walk forward now, along the veranda and in through the french windows, she would find herself inside the other Ardilla, within the rooms that did not exist except in dreams.

She wanted to go forward, but she was afraid.

Her mother turned a page. The wind chimes tinkled. A bird called from the beach.

Jen looked away, out over the paddock. When she looked back her perception was normal again. Everything looked as it always did. Except . . . except there was a slight flicker in the corner of her eyes that suggested something was there where nothing should be.

She shook herself mentally like a wet dog and decided to go and swim. She took her bathers from the clothes hoist outside the back door, changed into them in the bathroom and walked down to the beach.

Sally and Mrs Melville were sitting talking under the

beach umbrella, and everyone else was in the water. Mr Fraser and Mr Melville were standing waist deep, chatting, while the children swam around them, splashed them, hurled themselves on top of them and tried to get them to retaliate. Every now and then one of the men, usually Mr Fraser, would lazily pursue the attackers and give them a good ducking. Jen's father was perched on a rock, looking dark and solitary like a cormorant.

Sally stretched her arms over her head and yawned. "Nicky woke me up so early," she said to Mrs Melville. "He was full of some dream he'd had about a big black bird in the cellar. There isn't a cellar in the house, though, is there?"

Jen didn't look at Sally. She was upset because Mrs Melville, one of her favourite people, was chatting to her in such a friendly way. The flicker behind her eyes seemed to be turning into a full-scale headache. She kicked off her thongs and dropped her towel. Then she walked straight down to the water.

Nicky was playing on the edge with a bucket and spade. He emptied out the bucket with a splash. Then he smacked it with his spade. "Naughty girl," he said. "Smack naughty girl."

"Who's a naughty girl?" Jen said.

"You naughty girl!" And he smacked the bucket again. "You chased Nicky with the big black bird!"

"Get lost!" she said, and dived into the water. His comment unnerved her. Why had he decided she was a naughty girl? Had someone told him she was? Sally and Mark, I suppose, she thought. Creeps, the pair of them!

Surfacing near Tom, she called to him, "Race you to the island!"

She had a head start, but he overtook her and got to

the island a full couple of minutes before she did.

"Woo!" she said, coming up, gasping, and pulling herself cautiously on to the rough rocks. "You been training or something?"

"Yeah, I'm in the district team this year. I've been doing laps three times a week."

"It shows!"

"You should do it too!"

"I don't have time!"

He nodded and grinned sympathetically. It was the first time they had been alone together this holiday. Was it going to be easy to assume their old familiar roles? Tom had never talked much, but they used to think about the same things. She hoped they still did.

"Should have brought the masks," he said now, peering down into the clear water. A dark shape flashed through and disappeared behind a rock. Tom gave a snort of satisfaction.

"Is that the first one you've seen? What was it?"

"Yup. Snapper, I think. We'll go snorkelling later and have a proper look. You seen your cormorant yet? 'Cos he's right up there if you haven't."

Jen shaded her eyes with her hand and looked up at the cormorant on the rock. "It was the first thing we saw when we did the Look."

"Oh, you did the Look? I thought you might have forgotten. I didn't like to ask with . . . you know, them, around . . ." His voice trailed away, and there was a trace of embarrassment in it.

"D'you think it's all a bit babyish this year?"

Tom shrugged, still gazing down into the deep clear water.

"I used to think it was what kept Ardilla standing from

year to year," Jen said, looking across at the house. "I thought if we didn't do the Club one year the house wouldn't be there the next."

"You think a lot of weird things when you're a little kid," Tom said slowly. "I used to have to count all the knives and forks when I was setting the table. If I didn't, I thought the food would poison us."

"And you don't do that any more?"

"Nah! Grew out of it!"

And he's grown out of the Club, Jen thought. But I don't think I have. Or is it really something you can grow out of?

The cormorant gave a loud croak, as if in warning.

Jen was cold and her head was still aching. "I think I'll go back," she said, and sat up.

Little sunspots danced darkly on the periphery of her vision. The cormorant gave another croak of alarm and flew off. Jen blinked to clear her eyes, and when she opened them again, Sally was in front of her. She was kneeling in the bow of the dinghy, preparing to jump on to the rocks. Mr Fraser was at the oars, and Mark was perched in the stern.

"Ah," Mr Fraser said in his maddening joky voice. "'The common cormorant or shag, Lays eggs inside a paper bag!'"

"Great place!" Sally exclaimed, landing lightly beside Tom. "You're burning," she told him. "You want me to put some oil on you? I brought mine over with me."

He turned even pinker. "I'm going back now," he muttered, and slid into the water.

Sally laughed. "Oh, scared him off! Shame! He's rather cute, isn't he, Jennifer? Is he your boyfriend?" She emphasised the last syllable—Jenni*fer*. It sounded horrible.

"Nooo!" Jen said scornfully. "He's just a friend."

"'The reason for this fact, no doubt,'" Mr Fraser continued to recite, while helping Mark out of the boat, "'Is to keep the lightning out!'"

"We have to wear lifejackets in the dinghy," Jen told him, hoping to shut him up. She hated the silly rhyme about cormorants. Her cormorant was a magic bird, a totem, and she didn't want anyone making a fool out of it.

"A very sensible rule too," Mr Fraser agreed. "Your dad's gone up to the house to fetch them. But just this once, since it's as flat as a pancake, both the kids can swim like fish, and I'm a former Iron Man champion, I figured we could break the rule. Rules are made to be broken, aren't they, especially when you're on holidays!"

It sounded rather subversive to Jen. She wasn't sure if she liked adults who thought breaking rules was a good idea. But Mr Fraser didn't behave like a proper adult really. She wondered if that was what happened to you when you got divorced—or perhaps that was why his wife had gone away. She suspected Mr Fraser would have preferred to be one of the kids. He didn't behave much like a father, even to Nicky. Sally took more care of the little boy than he did. Even out here on the island, Sally kept looking back to check that Nicky was still safely at the edge of the water, waving to him when he looked across at her. Tom had stopped next to him and was helping him build a sandcastle.

"I'm going back too," Jen said.

"Hop in!" Mr Fraser said. "I'm the ferry service today!"

"It's all right, I'll swim." Before he could argue, Jen

slipped into the water and headed for the shore.

When she got there her father was back with the lifejackets and was staring out at the Frasers. Mr Fraser was playing what looked like a game of pirates with his two older children. He had threatened to maroon them and was rowing away. They stood and hurled insults at him from the rocks.

Mr Gilroy was frowning, the groove of tension deep between his eyes.

"I told him they should have worn lifejackets," Jen said, wrapping herself up in her towel. She was cold again.

"Yes, well, I suppose he knows what he's doing," her father said, not sounding too happy about it. "I guess it doesn't matter for once, as long as he's with them."

But when the Frasers finally returned he had a quiet word with Mr Fraser. Mr Fraser's reply was not quiet at all. "You need to relax, Tony, old mate. Don't worry so much. This is meant to be a holiday, right? The kids need to run wild a bit. Does 'em good."

"Yes, of course," Mr Gilroy replied mildly. "But there are certain rules which . . ."

"We won't do it again. Scouts' honour!" Mr Fraser grinned broadly and slapped Jen's father on the shoulder. "Now we've got the jackets, who's ready for a longer trip?"

Mark and Richy immediately clamoured to go.

"I'll come," Lisa said, not wanting to be left behind.

"Room for one more?"

"I'm staying with Nicky now," Sally said. The little boy came up just then, saying excitedly, "Nicky go in boat? Daddy take Nicky in boat?"

"Better not, old son," Mr Fraser said. "You can't

37

swim at all."

Nicky's face crumpled and he opened his mouth.

"Don't cry, Nicky," Sally pleaded. "I'll take you back for lunch. You're hungry, aren't you."

He shook his head and said, through tears, "Go in boat!"

"That's enough, mate! Don't be such a sook!" Mr Fraser said impatiently. "I'm not taking you out and that's that. What about you, love?" he said to Jen.

"I've got a headache," she said. "I think I'll go back to the house."

"There you are," Mr Fraser said to Jen's father. "That kid's under too much pressure. Headaches! At twelve years old! Doing her music practice on the first day of the holidays! You need to let up, love. Learn to relax. Don't let your old man drive you too hard. He'll have you suffering from migraine next."

Jen's father looked at her in concern. "Are you all right? Do you want me to come back to the house with you?"

"I'm fine," she said between her teeth. She was furious with Mr Fraser for voicing one of her fears. She had a sudden vision of her father's bad days, when he could only lie, not moving, in a darkened room. Migraine was like a family curse. She didn't want it passed on to her. "I'm probably just hungry."

She tried to sound casual and cheerful, and she must have succeeded, for the two men stopped looking at her and she was able to leave the beach on her own. Nicky was calmed down by having a little ride in the boat in shallow water, and then Tom joined the others for the trip with Mr Fraser. Jen walked up to the house. When she got to the paddock wall, she turned and looked out over the bay. The dinghy was beyond the island and Mr Fraser was rowing with clean strong strokes.

She wished he wasn't so good at it. She wished he would make a mistake, or something would happen to wipe the grin off his face. With a father like that, no wonder Sally and Mark were such creeps.

5

On hot afternoons at Ardilla the parents usually took long siestas or read in the south-facing dining-room, and the children played in the shade or in the outbuildings, but after lunch the indefatigable Mr Fraser was restless and proposed a trip down to Frewin Bay.

"We can pick up some bait while we're there, eh, Mark?"

"Oh, you're planning to do some fishing," Mr Melville said with interest. "That'll be good for the kids. You'd like to do some fishing, wouldn't you, Richy?"

Jen waited to hear him deny it, but Richy exclaimed, "Yeah, that'd be great!"

No one else made any protest either. Mr Melville went on, "Nothing like fresh grilled snapper. Or you might get some whiting if you're lucky."

"Yum," Richy said happily. "I love whiting. Can we go when we get back from the Bay?"

Jen hissed to Tom, "You're not going to go fishing with them, are you?"

He shrugged. "Why not? Might be fun."

"It's your totem!"

"But I've always eaten fish," Tom replied, looking puzzled.

"Yeah, but you haven't gone out and killed them here at Ardilla."

"Doesn't Jennifer approve of fishing?" Mr Fraser said, with a wide grin.

"We've never been fishing here," she replied boldly. "We don't like killing things unnecessarily. I think fishing is horrible."

"Quite the little greenie, aren't we!" he laughed. "I don't mind betting you'll eat it when you smell it sizzling in the pan!"

"I won't eat anything you catch," she retorted in a low voice.

"Rather warm to go out, isn't it?" her father said. Jen wasn't sure if he was coming to her rescue or not, but she was grateful to him for taking the attention away from her. The adults were starting to look at her with those infuriating smiles that said something like, "Isn't she funny to care so much. It's quite sweet, really—as long as it's not going to inconvenience us in any way!"

"The Merc's air-conditioned," Mr Fraser replied. Once he'd got an idea in his head he'd never be persuaded to give it up, Jen realised, looking at him with dislike.

"Why don't I take all the kids?" he was saying. "Give you lot a break?"

"You can't fit them all in, can you?" Mrs Melville asked.

"No sweat! They can all squeeze in the back. The Merc's as big as a hearse!"

"What about seatbelts?" Mrs Gilroy sounded a bit anxious.

"Di, you worry too much! I haven't had an accident in twenty-five years' driving. They'll be perfectly all right! Who's for a little trip, kids? Take you all down to the Bay and get you ice creams, eh? While the olds put their feet up and cop some zees!"

Jen had pretended to eat some lunch, but the food tasted all wrong. The idea of the Frasers going fishing at Ardilla revolted her. Her head was pounding and the thought of a drive in the car made her feel sick. She definitely didn't want to go, and she didn't want Lisa, Tom and Richy to go either. She tried to make signs at them to stay—for then they could have the afternoon to themselves without the Frasers—but they were all jumping round Mr Fraser as if he was the Pied Piper. The prospect of a ride in the Mercedes was too tempting, quite apart from the promise of ice creams in the Bay. The only person who noticed her was Mr Fraser, and she turned quickly away in case he winked at her again.

"What about you, sweetheart?" he called, in a fake Cockney accent like someone from *EastEnders*, as everyone else ran to get ready. "You fancy a spin in my motor?"

She shook her head.

"Why don't you go?" her father said, perhaps remembering the conversation on the beach.

"I don't feel like it," she said, getting up from the table. She whispered to her mother as she went past, "I've got a headache, Mum. I think I'll go and lie down for a bit."

Mr Fraser overheard. "Poor Mistress Jen," he said, parodying her whisper. "A touch of the vapours, I fear."

She wanted to yell something really rude at him but she had been brought up to be polite to adults, so she simply gave him a poison-filled look as she left the room.

She heard him say, as she went slowly up the stairs, "I don't think I've hit it off with madame!"

Her mother's voice came more faintly. "She takes time to get used to things. I'm afraid she's very temperamental."

"I'd call it moody! I reckon her ladyship's nose has been put out of joint by my Sally!"

Burning with resentment, which made her head hurt more and more, Jen crossed Neutral Ground and went into the little bedroom. Sally was leaning over the make-up mirror she had brought with her, putting on lipstick. Her reflected eyes met Jen's.

"You coming?"

"No," Jen said, throwing herself down on her bed.

There was a slight pause as Sally dabbed her lips with a tissue.

"Good!" she said, and left the room.

Jen clenched her fists and her teeth. So Sally didn't like her either. She was surprised to realise that she minded a bit. Some strange part of her wanted Sally to like and admire her. But Sally didn't want her around. Well, stuff her then! She thumped her pillow with her fist, trying to let out some of her rage.

She heard the others' voices faintly outside, and the sound of the engine as the car raced away down the driveway—much faster than either her father or Mr Melville ever drove. Perhaps he'll have an accident, she thought. He'll be terribly injured, and the kids will have to go back to Melbourne. She pictured herself looking at him as he lay in a hospital bed, but even lying in a plaster cast, he winked at her. She tried to shut her mind to him altogether.

It was hot under the roof, and the room did not seem like the refuge it had always been before—probably because Sally's gear was all over it. The red-smudged tissue still lay on the floor. Disgusting, Jen thought. She was lying wondering if she would get up and find somewhere cooler or if she would try and go to sleep, wishing her head did not hurt so much, almost sorry she had not gone with the others, when she heard the sound of footsteps on the stairs, and her mother looked in.

"Just came to see if you were all right."

"I've got such a bad headache."

"Do you feel sick too?"

"I don't know. Not really. I just feel kind of funny. Everything tastes wrong, and everything looks wrong too."

"Oh dear! It does sound like migraine."

"It's not," Jen said at once, desolated by the thought. "It's just a headache. I was probably out in the sun too much this morning."

"It wouldn't have anything to do with the Frasers, would it?" Mrs Gilroy came in and sat on the end of Jen's bed. "You aren't just making yourself sick because you think you don't like having them here?"

"I *don't* like having them here! Oh Mum . . .!"

"Jennifer!" her mother interrupted pleadingly.

Jen was silent. She had been about to attempt to say what she really felt, but her mother was not going to allow her to go on. Her mother only wanted her to be kind and nice and to love having other people around, especially if it was doing them a good turn. She was not really interested in how Jen was feeling, and Jen knew she would never be able to explain it to her. She was already half ashamed of the way she felt: she didn't want to see her mother's disappointment and shock as well. She rolled over and said, "It's so hot up here!"

"Come down and lie on my bed, and I'll get you some ice for your head. It always makes Dad feel better. If it's still bad later I'll go down to the Bay and try and find

Doctor Allen. He might be able to give you something."

I am standing at the top of the steps that lead down into the cellar beneath Ardilla. The real Ardilla has no cellar, but I am in the other Ardilla, the one that lies beneath the surface, the one that is going to emerge. I think with relief that Sally and Mark will never find us here, that we can hold the Club meetings down here in the cellar beneath Ardilla that no one knows about, but then I remember that we will not be doing the Club any more. Something has happened to break the spell that bound us to Ardilla. Our links with the totems are broken.

It is with fear that I descend into the shadows. Dead fish, birds' skeletons, the broken claws of crabs crunch under my feet. Beyond the passageway I know there are many large, light, beautiful rooms, but I cannot get to them because something of impenetrable darkness blocks the way. I can see its huge beaked head. I feel the air rush past my face as it beats its black wings. Beneath its feathers I can see its bones. It opens its mouth and shrieks at me.

Jen awoke with a start, the echoes of the shriek still in her ears. It had been cooler in her parents' room and the ice pack had taken the edge off the pain in her head. Sleepy after her restless night, she had dozed off. For a moment she did not know where she was. She sat up swiftly, aware of some urgency within her, something terribly important she had to do, something to do with the weird dreams.

The sun, southwesterly now, was touching the edge of the window. It was late afternoon. The leaves of the trees around the house threw little pinhole images of the sun on the walls and floor. The sound came again, followed a moment later by the noise of an engine. The shriek that had wakened her was the blaring horn of the Mercedes. At that moment the car came to a screaming halt outside.

Jen got carefully off the bed. The headache had receded—perhaps that meant it wasn't migraine, for she knew her father's headaches persisted for two days or more. From the wide window seat of the bedroom, half concealed by the heavy curtains, she could see the other children as they jumped out of the car.

"Twenty-two minutes, thirty seconds," Tom shouted excitedly to Mr Fraser, proudly showing him his stopwatch.

"Crawling!" Mr Fraser replied, laughing. "I reckon we should be doing it in eighteen! We'll have another shot at the record tomorrow, right?"

"Right!" they all chorused. They looked suspiciously like a gang to Jen as they ran chattering and laughing into the house. And she was the outsider, watching them like a spy through the curtains, unable simply to run and join them. Tom, Richy, even her sister, Lisa, seemed suddenly drawn away from her. No matter what she did or said when she came out of the bedroom, Mr Fraser would be watching her. And he would call her "her ladyship" or "Mistress Jen"! And everybody would laugh because they would politely pretend he was being funny, whereas he was being cruel to her, Jen knew it.

He doesn't like me, she thought. It didn't surprise her. Many adults didn't like her. They found her too intense and difficult.

That's fine! He doesn't like me and I don't like him. And I don't like his horrible kids. And if he goes fishing here I'll never forgive him. I'll pay him out for it somehow. I'll get back at him.

That's what the bird wants. That's what the bird is saying. If the totems are ignored and betrayed, someone must pay. And the bird is mine. I am the bird's. If the bird is placated I can go into the heart of the other Ardilla.

With the image of the cormorant clear in her mind, Jen fetched her flute from the sitting-room and went back to her parents' bedroom. There she found that she could lose herself in playing. For a long time the haunting music echoed plaintively round Ardilla, as the sun set and everyone else played riotous and noisy games with Mr Fraser.

6

The next few days followed the same pattern. Sally kept an eye on Nicky and chatted with the adults. Tom, Richy and Mark formed a sort of "boys only" gang, grudgingly allowing Lisa to tag along. Mr Fraser took them out fishing and their conversation became full of discussions about whiting, tommy ruffs, dabs, and the best sort of bait for each. Mr Melville cooked with enthusiasm whatever they caught. Jen refused to eat it.

She often found herself alone, walking on the beach, floating on her back in the warm water, deep inside her own head, thinking her own thoughts.

She felt much younger than Sally and yet much older than the other four children. Even Tom, who was only one day younger, seemed to be years behind her. She realised that there was no one else like her anywhere in the world. No matter how many other people there were, not one would ever be the same as she was. The thought made her feel dizzy, as she did when looking at the vastness of the night sky and the infinite number of stars, but it also made her feel strong.

She spent a lot of time playing the flute. She mastered the tricky bit in the Handel sonata and started work on the Bach Partita in A minor. It was impossibly hard, but it gave her something to concentrate on, and having to practise became an excuse to get away from Sally.

After days of hot weather a cool change came through one night. Rain fell briefly, tapping like birds' claws on the roof. The roof leaked, and Lisa woke up with a wet bed. It was still cold and showery in the morning, and a fresh southerly was stirring the sea into choppy waves.

"If it rains all day we won't get any dinner," Mr Melville said at breakfast. "All the saucepans are catching drips!"

"We'll have to talk to the agents about the roof," Jen's father said. "The whole place is going to fall down if they don't do some repairs."

"Who does Ardilla belong to?" Mark asked, pouring cereal into a bowl and spilling most of it on the floor.

"Mrs Fairlie-Jones. She's a sort of cousin of Tony's," Mrs Gilroy replied, getting up from the table to get a dustpan and brush.

"Very distant and several times removed," Mr Gilroy added. "I think she's in a home now, poor old dear. She must be about ninety. She lived here when she was a child, while the land was still being farmed."

"You know what I'd do with it, if it was mine?" Mr Fraser said. "Di, don't do that for Mark, make the lazy kid do it himself. Pull the whole place down and make a beach resort. Perfect spot for it!"

Jen stared at him in horror. Was he joking? She looked at her father. He shot a glance back at her, and shook his head ruefully.

"We like it how it is," he stated. "If I bought it I'd keep it just like this."

"Apart from fixing the roof," Lisa laughed.

Dad doesn't like Mr Fraser either, Jen thought. He's sorry he asked him! Huh! He should have listened to me in the first place. She gave her father a slight smile.

"I think it's lovely how it is too," Mrs Melville said, pretending to be shocked. "You're a bit of a Philistine, aren't you, Joe!"

"I hate to see things going to waste," he replied. "I'd like to see more people getting some use out of this place."

"More people!" Mr Gilroy said with a shudder. "The place is crawling with people—especially kids! I'm sure we've got more than we came with! Which one was yelling in the middle of the night?"

"It was Nicky," Sally said.

"Was it?" her father said in surprise. "I didn't hear him."

"Dad, once you're asleep, you don't hear anything. I had to get up and go to him."

"What was wrong, did he have a wet bed too?" Mr Fraser laughed heartily.

"No, he had a bad dream, didn't you, Nicky?"

Nicky put his spoon down and nodded seriously. "Big black bird," he said. "In a bad place under the house."

"Very nasty!" Mr Melville said.

"Does he often have nightmares?" Mrs Melville enquired.

"No, it's only since we've been here."

"Probably just the change, being in a strange place," Mrs Gilroy said.

"Tom, don't take the last of the orange juice," Richy shouted at his brother. "Geez, Mum, I haven't had any yet!"

"Here," Mark said, "you can finish mine." He pushed his glass across to Richy, spilling some of what was in it on the way.

"Steady on, Mark, you clumsy git!" Mr Fraser

growled.

Mr Gilroy cast his eyes up to the ceiling and groaned.

"Don't take any notice of him," Mrs Gilroy said, pouring herself another cup of coffee. "He's a misanthropist!"

"There's one thing you can say about Tony." Mr Melville joined in the teasing. "He's not racist. He just hates everyone!"

"I'm very selective!" Mr Gilroy retorted. He got up to get a cloth, and wiped up the orange juice. Mark and Richy were giggling.

"Too selective," said Mrs Gilroy. "You could be a bit more friendly, you know."

"Has anyone got any plans today?" Mr Gilroy changed the subject. He threw the cloth into the sink and stared out of the window as another squall of rain blew in from the sea. "It's going to be too rough to take the boat out."

"I hope the weather clears up," Mrs Gilroy said. "I don't know what the children will do if they're stuck indoors all day. And I've got those sheets to dry too."

"Don't worry about it, Di!" Mr Fraser said cheerfully, spreading large quantities of marmalade on his toast.

It was a phrase he seemed to be using a lot, Jen thought. He was always telling someone not to worry about things. He should worry, she thought. He should worry about being such a creep and having such creepish children!

"I'll take the kids out for the day," Mr Fraser went on. "What say I take them all down to the Bay for lunch? Fish and chips at Don's Diner? Who's on?"

All the children except Jen cheered.

"Get your skates on, then! Leaving at ten hundred hours!"

"Can we have another shot at the record?" Richy said eagerly.

"Sssh!" Mr Fraser put his finger to his lips and looked round with exaggerated caution. "Enemy spies abound. Your mothers will have a heart attack!" He began to tiptoe away to the door, followed by the giggling children, but then he turned and said to Jen, "What about your ladyship? Will you grace us with your company today?"

She was going to say no, but her mother answered for her. "Of course she'll go, it'll do her good."

"Deeply honoured," Mr Fraser said with a sweeping bow, but Jen saw Sally's face behind him and caught the grimace of annoyance Sally made.

Stuff her! she said to herself. I'll go just to spite her!

"OK," she said. "I suppose it's something to do."

Mr Fraser winked at her and grinned.

In the car the boys and Lisa, squashed in the back seat, wriggled and squealed with excitement. Jen had to share the front seat with Sally, who held Nicky on her knee. It was a bit too close to Mr Fraser for her liking. She could smell his after-shave. His hands looked very large on the steering-wheel.

"Ready!" he shouted over the clamour from the back seat.

"Get set," Mark said, and "Go!" they all yelled together.

The car leaped forward, gravel spitting from its wheels, and tore down the driveway. The pine trees flashed past. In a few seconds they were out on the bitumen road, where they narrowly missed a truck as they turned. Jen gasped. She'd never been so fast in a car.

"Slow down!" she said to Mr Fraser. She didn't like it. It was frightening.

"Don't worry," he said, taking his eyes off the road for what seemed like five minutes. "I've never had an accident. I'm a very good driver! Aren't I, Sal?"

"You're a maniac," his daughter replied, laughing. He took that as a huge compliment and laughed too.

"Faster! Faster!" Nicky chortled from Sally's knee. The car took a curve. The road stretched straight ahead to the Bay. Mr Fraser put his foot down.

Jen shut her eyes. She felt as though she was being hurled through space. She could see horrible images, like those she had sometimes seen on the news, of them all smashed to pieces under a truck.

"Don't you like it?" Sally said in her ear.

She opened her eyes. "It's OK," she lied, not wanting the others to think she was being a wimp. "But isn't it a bit risky, breaking the speed limit? Suppose the cops get you?"

Mr Fraser tapped a gadget on the dash. "This is my little anti-radar device. Gives me a bit of warning. Anyway, the police should be out catching the real crims, not hassling good drivers like me. That's what I always tell 'em!"

Jen did not know what to reply to this. She knew he was wrong, and driving dangerously, but her parents had told her to go with him and she knew they wanted her to be polite to him. And she could hardly tell him to stop the car so she could get out!

Luckily the journey was a short one.

"Twenty minutes, ten seconds!" Tom exclaimed as the car slowed down at the 60k speed limit sign.

"Not bad!" Mr Fraser said. "We're getting there!"

"We're trying to set a record," Lisa explained to Jen, hanging over the back of the seat. "From the speed limit sign to Ardilla."

Jen said nothing, but when they were out of the car and walking down the street she pulled Lisa away from the others and whispered, "I bet Mum and Dad don't know about it. They wouldn't like it if they did!"

"They don't have to know about it," Lisa said, her blue eyes large and innocent. "We do a lot of things that they don't know about. Like the Club. They've never known about that, and they wouldn't like us climbing on the roof—but we still do it! Don't tell them," she added. "They might not let us go out with the Frasers, and that'll cause trouble."

"Perhaps the Frasers'd leave then?" Jen said hopefully.

"I don't mind them being here," Lisa said. "I think it's fun having them." Then she spotted the boys heading off without her. "Wait for me," she yelled, and tore after them.

"Meet you at Don's at twelve!" Mr Fraser's yell was even louder than Lisa's, so loud that several people in the street turned to stare. It didn't bother Mr Fraser at all. He gave everyone who looked at him a broad grin and went on talking rather too loudly, as though he knew he was the centre of attention and liked it.

"Nicky, my old mate, you come with me. I'm going to get you a surprise! Give your sister a bit of a break. She probably wants to go and chat up the boys on the beach! If she takes you they'll think she's an unmarried mother!"

"Daad!" Sally protested, but she was smiling too and she gave her father a friendly dig in the ribs.

"Take Mistress Jen with you and see if you can get

her to let her hair down!" He took hold of Jen by the shoulders and gave her a bit of a push towards Sally.

"Come on," Sally said. She must have noticed how Jen froze when Mr Fraser touched her, for as they crossed the street and began to walk towards the sea, she went on, "Don't mind Dad. He just likes teasing people. He doesn't mean anything."

They walked slowly past the shops, stopping now and then to look at earrings or T-shirts, shells and other souvenirs.

"It drives Mum demented," Sally said, not looking at Jen. It was the first time she had mentioned her mother. "But she doesn't know how to handle Dad. I get along with him heaps better than she does."

Jen wanted to say something back, but she couldn't think of anything. Should she tell Sally she hated the way Mr Fraser winked at her? Should she say something sympathetic about the fact that Sally's parents were divorced? She had a sudden sharp memory of how sad Sally had looked the first evening when she had watched her outside Ardilla. She pretended to be studying a rack of fluorescent T-shirts. *Fun at Frewin Bay!* they proclaimed.

"Gross," Sally said beside her. "I wouldn't wear that if you paid me!" Then she dropped her voice almost to a whisper. "These earrings aren't bad, though. I wouldn't mind them."

She pointed out a pair of earrings to Jen. They were hand-crafted from beach-combed materials, set in gold. They were very attractive and looked expensive.

"Course, you haven't got pierced ears, have you?" Sally went on.

"Mum and Dad don't like them," Jen said.

Sally made an expressive face and shook her head.

"Hello, dear," a woman called from inside the shop. "Back again for the holidays?"

"Oh, hi, Mrs Weston," Jen replied, stepping in to talk to her. Over the years they had come to know many of the shopkeepers in Frewin Bay quite well. Mrs Weston was a pleasant-faced middle-aged woman who painted landscapes, gave art classes and sold her pictures and other souvenirs in the shop.

"Is that your sister outside?"

"No, it's a girl who's staying with us this year. Her name's Sally Fraser."

"Ah." Mrs Weston put on her glasses and studied Sally through them. Sally was examining the earrings carefully, holding them up against her ears and looking at herself in the tiny mirror on the top of the stand. She kept shooting glances towards the inside of the shop.

Mrs Weston made a face that could have meant almost anything. "How's the music coming along?" she asked.

"OK," Jen said. "Pretty good really. I'm going to be in high school next year, you know."

"Well," Mrs Weston said, "rather you than me!"

Jen laughed. She liked Mrs Weston. "How's the painting?"

"That's pretty good too, I think. Come out the back and I'll show you some of my latest ones."

They went through the curtain that hung at the back of the shop and out to the shed where Mrs Weston did her painting. Jen looked at the landscapes around the walls.

"That's Ardilla!" she said. "But in the winter."

"Yes, I did that last year. I wanted to capture it before . . ."

"Before what?"

"Before anything happens to it. You can never tell with these old places. So many of them have gone from round here. There's more development happening all the time." She sighed, looking sad. "Oh well. Better get back to the shop—you wouldn't believe how much stuff I've lost this summer."

"Lost?" Jen said, not understanding.

"Stolen. Shoplifted. I've never had such a bad year. There are more people coming to the Bay all the time. It doesn't improve it."

"No," Jen agreed. "It doesn't."

When she walked out of the shop, Sally was further down the street. She waved frantically to Jen and shouted to her, "Come on!"

Jen caught up with her. Sally grabbed her arm and hurried her round the corner.

"What's the rush?" Jen said. "Where're we going?"

"This gorgeous boy just went past. I saw him last time we were here. Let's follow him down to the beach!"

Away from Ardilla and without the responsibility of Nicky, Sally was looking pretty gorgeous herself, Jen thought with something like envy. It was unfair that anyone should be quite so pretty and have such smart clothes. She realised that she herself, in her old shorts and jumper, looked like a kid, whereas Sally, complete with her Sportsgirl shoulder bag and a sun visor she didn't really need as it was still cloudy, looked practically grown-up.

It was puzzling that she did not like Sally at all and yet she envied her, as if she wanted to *be* like her.

They went along the beachfront, under the row of Norfolk Island pines, Sally commenting on every boy they passed. Like her father, she acted as though she was the centre of everyone's attention. She talked a little bit too loudly, and danced along, making sweeping gestures with her sun visor, touching her lips with her tongue and smiling a lot.

"Here he comes," she hissed, giving Jen a sharp nudge.

As the gorgeous boy passed them, she gave him a brilliant smile and said, "Hi!"

"Hi!" he replied appreciatively.

Sally dug Jen in the ribs again as they walked on. "Wasn't that great! Isn't he a spunk? He said hi to me!"

"So what?" Jen said, turning and watching the boy walk away.

"Don't look!" Sally said, pulling her round. "Never look as if you're too interested!"

"I don't think he was too interested," Jen said. "You'll probably never see him again. Anyway, you don't know who he is!"

"Oh, how terrible! I don't know who he is! I haven't been introduced!" Sally teased. "You don't know a thing about boys, do you?"

When Jen didn't answer, she went on, " You have to take things slowly. Just say hi a few times. Then you start talking. The thing is, he said hi back. He noticed me. Next time he'll be interested—they always are."

She said it with such complete confidence that Jen couldn't help being impressed. The boy did look nice. She liked the way his hair was cut and the way he had smiled. She wondered how she would have felt if he had smiled at her like that. If she carried on like Sally, would boys start noticing her? Did she want them to?

She grinned to herself.

"You should smile more often," Sally said. "You've no idea how different you look when you're not scowling.

Almost pretty. Well, pretty's not the right word. Attractive. Striking."

Jen stopped smiling at once and started scowling again.

Sally laughed. "Come on. Let's see if we can spot him once more and then we'll go and have lunch. You never know, he might have a friend for you!"

"Get away," Jen said. "I'm not interested."

"Everyone's interested," Sally said. "Sooner or later."

7

Lunch at Don's Diner was extremely lively. Mr Fraser had bought Nicky a face mask and a tiny pair of flippers, which the little boy insisted on wearing all through the meal. Mark and Richy teased him, calling him Freddo the Frog Man, which Sally immediately changed to Froggo the Fred Man. They ate huge amounts of fish and chips, and Mr Fraser let them order as many drinks as they liked.

Sally was very animated. She told stories that made everyone collapse with laughter, teased Richy and Tom, played games with Nicky, bossed her father.

Jen ate chips, not talking much, but finding she was enjoying being one of the group again. Sally was including her in the jokes and the conversation, almost as if she had set out to charm her. It was hard not to be charmed. She was having fun, even though Mr Fraser laughed and talked so loudly that everyone in the café kept staring at them.

She didn't even mind the drive home. It seemed daring and exciting to race through the countryside, and she was as disappointed as the others when a crawling truck made them a whole two minutes slower than before.

As soon as they got back to Ardilla, Nicky demanded to be taken to the beach to try out his new mask.

"Isn't it a bit cold?" Sally said, pretending to shiver.

"But it's not raining. Please, Sally!"

"OK, OK! I'll just put my things upstairs," Sally said. "Then we'll go straight down. Are you coming?" she added to Jen.

"OK," Jen said, flattered in spite of herself. "I'll get my swimsuit."

"It's under your bed," Sally said. "I noticed it this morning."

They ran upstairs together. Sally threw her shoulder bag on the bed; it slipped off on to the floor, and a handful of things fell out. Jen knelt to pick them up, and on the floor in front of her saw the earrings Sally had been admiring outside Mrs Weston's shop.

"Where did these come from?" she said in a puzzled voice, holding them up.

Sally scooped them quickly out of Jen's hand. "I bought them."

"You did not!" Jen retorted. "I was with Mrs Weston all the time. You never even came into the shop."

Sally did not answer directly. She was smiling with pleasure, her eyes bright with excitement, just as she had been all through lunch.

"You took them, didn't you?" Jen said.

"Maybe I did, maybe I didn't," Sally said infuriatingly.

"You can't do that!"

"Who says I can't?"

"You could have bought them. You've got plenty of money. What'd you have to steal them for?"

Sally put the earrings away in her suitcase and locked it. "They'll always be special to me. I didn't just walk into that boring shop and buy them. I took a risk for them."

"That's Mrs Weston's shop, though. She's a friend of ours. You can't steal things from her!"

"What are you going to do about it? Make me take them back? Own up and all that? Don't make me sick! And don't pretend you've never done it. Everyone does it all the time."

Jen was silent. She knew a lot of kids from school who nicked things from shops—lollies, chocolate bars, pencils, that sort of thing. But she didn't know anyone who'd stolen anything as expensive as the earrings.

She had taken something once—a long time ago, when she was three or four. She couldn't remember it herself, but it had become a family joke. She had pocketed a little toy in a shop and shown it proudly to her mother when they got home. Her parents had scolded her and taken it back with apologies, but later everyone had laughed about it and called her Jen the Shoplifter. Perhaps it had made a deep impression on her—anyway, she had never stolen anything since.

"Come on, Sally!" Nicky called from the bottom of the stairs.

"You coming?" Sally said to Jen.

Jen shook her head.

Sally looked at her pityingly. "Geez, you're a square!"

She walked nonchalantly to the door, turned, and said, "You'd better not say anything to anyone else." Then she ran down the stairs. Jen heard her say to Nicky, "Come on, Froggo!" and heard Nicky's squeal of delight. Their footsteps echoed away.

She sat down on the bed, totally confused. She'd started to like Sally. It had been fun at lunch, being part of the group. She didn't want to be isolated again. But poor Mrs Weston. It wasn't fair on her. How could Sally do that? Everyone thought she was such a marvellous person, the adults all admired her so much, everyone liked her much more than they liked Jen. They didn't know what she was really like. And what on earth was Jen going to do about it? Should she tell someone? Would it be dobbing? Or should she just pretend nothing had happened?

There was a clatter on the stairs and Lisa burst into the room. "Hey!" she said. "Are you coming down to the beach?"

"Lisa," Jen said.

"Mm?" Lisa had her jumper over her head and her reply was muffled.

"I've got to tell someone something. If I tell you, will you absolutely promise not to tell a single soul?"

"Sure!" Lisa mumbled.

"Sally stole some earrings from Mrs Weston's shop."

Lisa's head popped clear. She pushed her hair out of her eyes. "No kidding! Wow, that's pretty risky! Didn't anyone see?"

It was not quite the shocked reaction Jen had expected. "No one saw her take them, but I saw the earrings just now. She stole them."

"Wow!" Lisa said again, as she pulled off her pants and struggled into her bathers. "Gross! These are still wet!"

"What do you think I should do?"

"I don't know! Are you coming or not? I'm ready!"

"Do you think I should tell Mum and Dad?"

"No way! You'll only upset them. You don't have to do anything. It's not your problem."

"I want to talk to Mum about it."

Lisa stopped at the doorway. "I don't think you should dob."

"But it's serious, Lisa. She stole something."

63

"Only a pair of earrings. They probably weren't worth much. Anyway, you shouldn't dob. It's not fair."

Jen was surprised that Lisa was standing up for Sally so strongly. "I think it was a terrible thing to do!" she burst out. "They're horrible kids!"

"Actually, I quite like them," Lisa said boldly. She gave her sister a defiant stare. "We all think you're being horrible, if you want to know. It's you that's spoiling the holiday, not them."

There was a yell from downstairs. "Wait for me!" Lisa yelled back. "Don't bother coming with us," she said to Jen. "It's more fun without you."

"I don't want to come with you, you creep!" Jen shouted rather weakly after her as Lisa disappeared. "I hate and despise the lot of you!" She sat down on the top stair, her eyes itching with angry tears.

A few seconds later her mother came out of her bedroom and stood at the foot of the stairs. She could not see Jen's face against the light. "You're back, are you? Did you have a nice time?"

"No!" Jen snarled.

"What's the matter? Is something wrong? I thought I heard some shouting. Are you kids all getting on together?"

"Oh sure!" Jen said. "That's why everyone's gone off without me and I'm sitting on my own here."

"Darling, I'm sure they didn't mean to go off without you." Mrs Gilroy came up the stairs and sat down beside Jen. "You could make more of an effort to join in, you know. Perhaps you are being a little stand-offish."

"Stand-offish?" It was not a word her mother used very often, and Jen immediately suspected that she was quoting someone else. "Who says I'm being stand-offish? It's Mr Fraser, isn't it. He's been talking to you about me. Calling me 'Mistress Jen' and 'her ladyship'. I wish he wouldn't, Mum. I hate it."

"Don't be silly, he's only teasing you. It's his way of being friendly!"

Jen looked at her mother closely. "Do you like him?"

"Well, yes, I do! He's a lot of fun. He shakes us all up a bit. We had got very staid, you know, always doing the same old things. It's been good for us all having the Frasers here."

Jen thought about this for a few moments. She realised that Mr Fraser had a special way of talking to her mother, teasing and flattering at the same time. And her mother liked it. She laughed back at him—last night she had even playfully swiped him with a damp tea-towel while they were washing up in the kitchen.

"Does Dad like him?"

"Oh, Dad doesn't like anyone!" her mother said sharply. "He's the one that really needs shaking up a bit."

Not wanting to hear any more of this, wanting to change the subject, Jen said, without really meaning to, "Sally stole something today!"

"Stole something? Something of yours? Don't worry, she'll give it back."

"No, something from a shop. Some earrings. She was outside Mrs Weston's shop, and I was inside talking to Mrs Weston, and when we came home I saw them. They fell out of her bag. And now she's locked them in her suitcase."

The story sounded weak even to Jen's ears.

"Jen! You mustn't make wild accusations like that!" Mrs Gilroy stood up swiftly. She seemed to tower above Jen. "You really are jealous of Sally. Joe was right."

Joe? She had to think for a moment who her mother meant. Of course, Mr Fraser's name was Joe.

"It's not fair!" Jen stood up too so she wouldn't feel so dwarfed. "I'm telling you what happened and you won't even listen to me."

"I don't want you making up stories that aren't true. Of course Sally wouldn't steal things. Why should she need to? They have plenty of money and she only has to ask her father . . ."

"I'm not making it up! She took the earrings and she didn't pay for them!"

"There's probably some perfectly simple explanation—you just misunderstood what was happening. I'll talk to her father and clear it up."

"No, don't!" Jen said, wishing she'd never mentioned the subject. Whatever happened, she didn't want Mr Fraser to know, and she didn't want Sally to know that she had told anyone. "Just forget it!" She pushed past her mother and went downstairs. "I'm going for a walk."

It was still cool and cloudy. From the paddock Jen could see the other children on the beach. Sally was in the water with Nicky, and the other four were playing cricket with Mr Fraser and Mrs Melville. She didn't feel like joining them. She wished she hadn't said anything to her mother—she should have known she wouldn't believe her. She looked back and saw Ardilla. Beneath the grey sky it looked as it did in Mrs Weston's painting, old and vulnerable.

It really is falling down, Jen thought sadly.

Oh, my magic place, what's happening to you and how can I protect you?

She walked along the beach to the headland and climbed out over the rocks. Along the open cliff breakers were pounding, throwing up clouds of spray. She sat there for a long time watching them, waiting and listening intently.

Tell me what to do. I will wait until I receive a sign from you. I can sit here forever. No one is going to come looking for me. I am alone. Just as you are alone. No one cares about you except me. They have all forsaken you and abandoned your creatures. But I am still here. I will do whatever is needed. Just give me a sign.

She was not sure what she was waiting for, but the afternoon felt full of meaning, as though something really important was going to happen. She was going to find something out. She didn't know what it was, but when it came she was sure she would recognise it. She kept scanning the beach and the sea, listening alertly for any unusual sound, turning her head from time to time so she could see round the full circle.

The bank of cloud remained across the sky, blotting out the sun. The wind freshened. Two black-backed gulls swung overhead, so close that she felt the beat of their wings. A school of dolphins passed by, far out to sea. Neither gull nor dolphin had ever been a totem of Ardilla. She did not think they had any message for her.

After a long time a shout came from behind her, making her look round suddenly. She listened. The shout came again, and a moment later her father appeared over the rocks.

"Just came to see if you were all right," he said, climbing rather clumsily towards her, his black hair feathery over his ears, his beaked nose tanned dark brown.

"I'm fine," she replied. "I just didn't feel like being with anyone."

"I hope that doesn't include me," he said as he sat down on the rock next to her.

"Nuh!"

"Are you feeling OK?"

"Uh-huh."

"No more headaches?"

"Not really."

He said, "I'd feel terrible if you'd inherited migraines from me. What a thing to pass on to a kid!"

"It wouldn't really be your fault. Anyway, it wasn't migraine. It was just a headache."

They sat in silence for a few minutes. Jen resumed her intent watch.

"Do you want to go back?" Mr Gilroy said.

"In a little while," she answered remotely. "I'm just waiting for something."

"What?"

"Oh, just something."

Jen could see the cormorant fishing from the rocks at the end of the island. "There you are," she said to it, inside her head. "Are you going to tell me what I'm looking for?"

Down on the beach Mr Fraser was getting ready to go out in the boat. Mark, Tom and Richy were all with him. Jen watched them, her face set and still.

"Wonder what they'll catch today!" Mr Gilroy said. "Probably their deaths with this wind blowing!"

"Their deaths?" Jen said, startled into turning towards him.

"Death of cold." He looked at her closely. "Just a saying."

"They are catching death!" Jen said fiercely. "That's what fishing is. The fish drown in the air, you know. They feel it. People think fish don't feel anything, but they do." She looked back at the boat, now in the water and heading towards the island. "I wish they would catch their deaths."

"That's a bit extreme," Mr Gilroy commented. "You've got to learn to live and let live, Jen."

She ignored him, staring at the people in the boat as though she was actually ill-wishing them, and at that moment the cormorant rose from the water with its raucous shriek and flew over their heads, making Mark duck. She heard him give a shout of surprise.

"Fascinating creatures, aren't they?" her father said, following her gaze. "Look at that!"

It wants them to go, Jen thought. It's telling me to get rid of them. But how am I going to do it?

The bird dived, surfaced and gulped, swallowing a fish.

"Very neat!" Mr Gilroy remarked. "He doesn't need to drive into Frewin Bay to get bait and then sit in a boat and dangle a hook in the water! Sometimes I think I prefer birds to people."

"I know I do!" Jen said with feeling.

"Look, I'm sorry you're not getting on very well with Sally Fraser. I really did think it was a good idea to invite them . . . I didn't realise it was going to cause so many problems." He fell silent, as if he was waiting for Jen to say something. She stared out to sea, hoping the boat would suddenly spring a leak and disappear. It wasn't her fault the Frasers had caused problems. She hadn't wanted them to come in the first place. She'd always known it was a terrible idea.

Her father went on rather awkwardly, "Your mother told me what you told her about Sally . . ."

"I also told her to forget the whole thing!" Jen said sullenly.

"She wasn't sure whether to believe you or not. I just wanted you to know that I believe you."

"She really did take them, Dad!" Jen was quite relieved to be able to talk about the theft with someone.

"I think she's a lot more disturbed than she lets on. That's why I think it's best if we just let it drop for now. The kids have had a rough time and they're just beginning to settle down. Let's not rock the boat, hey?"

"You mean we're not going to do anything about it?"

"Not for the time being. I'll have a word with her father, but privately."

"What about Mrs Weston? Why should she have to lose out? It's so unfair on her!"

"I'll have a chat with her too," Mr Gilroy said, looking more and more troubled. "I suppose I can straighten things out."

Jen looked at him. She wondered if he would really do anything about it or if he would just pretend it hadn't happened. "I don't think Sally's disturbed. I think she's plain horrible!"

Her father sighed. "You and she are just completely different types. You couldn't be expected to get on, I suppose."

"Why on earth did you ask them, Dad?"

"If it's any comfort to you, I'm beginning to regret I did!" Then, as though he was ashamed of having admitted it, he stood up. "Let's get back." He held out his hand to her and pulled her up. They scrambled over the rocks and back to the sand. Jen leaned on her father's hand and gave a hop and a skip, as she used to when she was little.

"Kids do some pretty strange things when their parents split up," he said.

"I hope you and Mum never split up!" Jen was feeling safer now that her father had believed her, safe enough to say things like that.

"I hope so too!" He put his arm round her and gave her one of his rare hugs. He was a shy and undemonstrative man and often seemed awkward with her, but at that moment she felt very close to him.

"I think we're a bit alike, aren't we, Dad?"

"In what ways, do you think?"

"Well, neither of us likes other people very much!"

He laughed. "I don't seem to have the knack of making friends like your mum does. But I hoped that was something, like migraine, that you wouldn't inherit from me!"

"It's good not to make friends too quickly," Jen said.

"Everyone needs friends," her father said. "But perhaps we need a few good ones, rather than a lot of shallow ones."

"Exactly! And you can't be friends with everyone, can you?"

"You probably won't make a lot of friends easily," Mr Gilroy said. "You've got too much talent and too strong a character. But not liking people is quite different from wanting to harm them."

"I just don't want them to harm me!" Jen defended herself.

And they must not harm the place I love.

8

A short while after Jen and her father had returned to the house, the fishing party turned up in great excitement.

"Look what we got!" Mark came bursting into the kitchen holding the bait bucket.

"Oh!" Mrs Melville exclaimed. "What a huge one! John'll be ecstatic!"

"Fresh crab for dinner," Mr Fraser said, beaming. "Just hope you've got a pot that'll hold this monster."

Jen looked into the bucket. The crab raised its claw threateningly and tried to run, scrabbling vainly on the plastic sides. Its eyes waved from side to side. It didn't like being in a bucket. It wanted to be back in the sea.

"Give that to me," Jen said, trying to grab the bucket from Mark. He held on to it firmly.

"Get away! It's mine. I caught it!"

"Yeah, and I'm going to put it back!"

"Jen," Mrs Melville said, "we can eat it. Crab is delicious."

"How are you going to cook it?" Jen demanded.

"Well, you boil them—but they don't feel anything."

"That's rubbish!" Jen shouted, still trying to pull the bucket away. "How can they be boiled alive and not feel anything?"

"You're such a sook," Mark said, in a superior way.

"Girls are like that," his father put in. "They can't help

it. Here, this saucepan should be big enough. Just drop the old beauty in here."

Jen looked wildly round. Wasn't anyone going to come to her defence? No, all of them were exclaiming over the crab, and looking forward to eating it!

"Did you get anything else?" Mr Melville had come into the kitchen. "I don't think that guy's going to feed the twelve of us, big as he is."

"Couple of tommies," said Mr Fraser. "We had something quite big on the handline, but Tom dropped it and it got away!"

"Yeah," Mark grumbled. "Lost the hook and all."

"Well, we'll boil the crab and make a seafood sauce with the fish!"

"Please don't boil the crab." Jen made one last plea to Mr Melville.

"Honey, we all eat living things. You've got to accept that. You eat chops and steaks and sausages, don't you? You can't make a fuss about the crab. It won't suffer, I promise you." He covered the crab with cold water and set the saucepan on the stove.

With anger and misery churning inside her, Jen suddenly realised she was going to throw up. She clapped her hand to her mouth and ran to the door.

The nausea continued all evening. Jen slept in her parents' bed, waking up at intervals to be sick into a bowl. Towards morning she fell into a light sleep and dreamed again of the Ardilla within.

I can't find my flute and I need to do my practising. When I ask the others if they've seen it, they turn away as if I'm invisible. I am running along the veranda at Ardilla, and it slopes away from me, distorted and treacherous. I drop

*on to my hands and knees and crawl along it, clinging
with my fingertips.*

*Then I hear the music. Someone is playing my flute
and playing it perfectly, every note of the Partita precise
and exquisite. I crawl along the veranda, towards the
sound of the music. It comes thin and clear from below.*

*Now I am going to descend into the cellar that lies
beneath Ardilla. This time I will reach the beautiful
rooms where my music is being played. But the steps are
darker and more dangerous than they were before. There
are more bones on them. My feet crunch through the
debris up to my ankles. I am almost paralysed with fear.*

*The bird looms before me. It opens its huge beak, but
it does not shriek. It cannot shriek because it is dying. I
watch in terror as it towers over me. Its eyes roll in despair
and fear. It is trying to speak to me. What is it trying to
say? It is asking me for help, but what can I do? What
have I left undone? I must prevent it from dying. But
surely it must die so I can go past it and follow the music
to its source. Grief and guilt rise together in my throat like
vomit. I must prevent it from dying, yet it must let me past.*

Jen woke up with a start. The bedroom was empty.
The blinds were still drawn, but the light outside was
bright and the room was already quite warm. For a few
moments she lay, disoriented and shaky, thinking about
the extraordinary dream. It had left her with a sense
of urgency, but what had it meant and what was she
supposed to do?

She sat up gingerly, hugging her knees under the thin
quilt, wondering if she was feeling better. She tried very
hard not to think about the crab. Just the idea of it
made her feel nauseated again. And the other kids had
eaten it and said how delicious it was! Even Richy! How

could they? How could they forget the totems of Ardilla so quickly?

That's what I must do, she thought. Even though no one else wants to do the Club any more. I'll have to do all the rituals on my own. I'll go up on the roof today and get out the things.

This idea comforted her a little. She began to feel better. The bird did not have to die. She could heal it and placate it by doing the rituals, and then everything would be all right.

She could almost feel the house sigh and stretch in approval. She lay back in bed and stretched too. Her parents' bed was a lot more comfortable than the ones upstairs in the attics. Outside, the sun was shining brightly and the birds were making their early morning racket. Jen closed her eyes and began to doze again.

She could hear something else, beneath the calls and songs of the birds. For a moment she thought she was dreaming again, but as she listened more carefully she recognised the liquid notes of her flute.

There was no doubt about it. Someone was playing it. Anger got her out of bed in a hurry and held up her wobbly legs as she wrapped her mother's robe round her and rushed out of the room.

"That's excellent!" she heard Lisa say, from the kitchen. "Play something else!"

The music started up again. *Jingle bells, jingle bells.*

Jen walked into the kitchen. The music stopped abruptly. Sally lowered the flute and smiled triumphantly over it at Jen.

"Who said you could touch my flute?" Jen said in rage. "Give it here! Give it back!"

"OK, OK!" Sally replied, not returning the flute, but

waving it over her head out of Jen's reach. "There's no need to get so worked up! I haven't hurt it. I know how to play. I learned for a couple of years until it got too boring!"

"She's pretty good!" Lisa commented, watching Jen closely to see how she was going to take it.

" 'Jingle Bells'!" Jen sneered.

"Hey, can I have a try?" Mark asked.

"No!" Jen snapped back, snatching the flute from Sally. "No one's to touch it. Don't ever do that again!"

"Ooohh!" Mark made an idiotic noise at her and rolled his eyes in mock fright. Lisa giggled.

Jen looked round at them. There was a curious atmosphere in the kitchen, as though everyone knew something she didn't. Mark and Sally were staring boldly at her. Lisa and Richy were watching the Frasers, while Tom was eating rice bubbles very busily. Nicky was sitting next to him, eating rice bubbles too.

"What's wrong with everybody?" Jen said. She was still angry about Sally taking her flute, and her voice came out harsher than she really wanted it to. For although she was angry with the others, she also felt a strong and rather surprising desire to be one of them. It was not pleasant to be standing on one side of the kitchen with everyone else ranged on the other side against her.

"There's nothing wrong with any of us," Sally replied, emphasising the "us", and giving the others a swift, sweeping glance that included them all in her circle. Her glance rested slightly longer than necessary on Tom, and when he looked up at her, she smiled at him with warm, conspiratorial eyes.

Jen was dismayed. Tom was her special friend. How dare Sally smile at him like that? How did she know how to smile like that anyway? Where did she learn these things? How come Sally knew so much more than she, Jen, did, when she was only a few months older?

"Tom," she said, almost pleading.

He turned towards her, and there was a moment when she thought he was going to smile at her in his old, kind way, and they would get up and go out of the room together, go and swim, walk for hours on the beach without talking much, explore the rocks, do all the things they had done in other years, before the Frasers came, before Ardilla was spoilt.

Sally began to sing, teasingly, "*Must have been love.*"

"Don't be so stupid!" Jen burst out.

Tom went bright red and turned his attention back to his rice bubbles.

"Give me some of those!" Lisa said, grabbing the packet off the table. "I'm starving!" She poured out a huge bowlful, sliced a banana on top and drowned the whole lot in milk.

The food looked gross to Jen, distorted and repulsive. She could smell the almost sour smell of the milk and the ripe, rotting odour of the banana. It immediately became the target for her simmering anger. She made a disgusted face at her sister. "No wonder you're so fat!"

"I am not fat!" Lisa replied, outraged.

"You're horrible to Lisa," Mark remarked. "I'm glad you're not my sister."

"I'm not horrible to her," Jen said, her voice rising. "And I'm glad you're not my brother. I'd rather die than have you as a brother."

"Sally's much nicer than you are," Mark said, unmoved.

These words cut Jen deeply, and more so because

the others did not immediately disagree with them. She knew all too well that to the outside world they would appear to be true. Everyone would agree that Sally was nicer than she was. Sally was not cross or difficult. Sally did not get into rages or black moods. Jen wanted to scream out that she was worth as much as Sally, that Sally was not any better than she was. But she couldn't put it into words. She waited in vain for one of the others, Lisa, Richy or Tom, to say something to defend her, but they were all silent.

"You are horrible to Lisa," Sally said, breaking the silence. "You're horrible to everyone. I suppose you think you're much better than everyone else just because you can play the stupid flute." She turned her warm look on to Lisa and said, "You don't deserve a sister like Lisa. I wish she was my sister!" Lisa smiled back in amazed gratitude.

"You're a thief!" The words almost exploded out of Jen's mouth. "You steal things! You want everything for yourself!"

"You're the one that wants everything for yourself," Sally returned coolly. "You didn't want us to come here. You're jealous because we're here and we're all having a good time. Better than before. I've heard your mother say so."

The house seemed to tilt around Jen. The floors sloped away from her. There was a tremor as if Ardilla had been stricken deep in its heart. It no longer belonged to her. Strangers had come and stolen it from her.

Mark was looking at her closely. "You look like a retard," he said. "I think you're a bit mental."

"Oh, she's all right," Richy said, trying to calm things down. He looked rather anxiously from Jen to Sally and back again. "Why can't we all be friends together?"

"I don't want to be friends with any of you," Jen shouted, beside herself with rage and terror as the house expanded and contracted around her. It seemed to be sending disjointed words to her from its depths. She put her hands to her head.

"Are you OK?" Richy asked. His voice seemed to be coming from a long way away. She couldn't hear what the house was saying.

"Shut up," she snarled at him, unfairly.

"Naughty girl!" Nicky, who had been quietly dabbling his fingers in a mug of hot chocolate and sucking them, suddenly put in. "She's a naughty girl, Sally," he told his sister seriously.

"Even Nicky knows," Sally said mockingly.

"Nicky doesn't know anything. None of you know anything! You're all morons, complete and utter morons!" Jen was shrieking at the top of her voice. Then she turned and ran out of the kitchen, almost colliding with Mr Fraser in the doorway.

"Ooh, temper, temper!" he said, wagging his finger at her.

She heard his voice as she escaped. "What's wrong with Mistress Jen? Has something else upset her ladyship?"

The trouble was, there was no escape from any of them. Everywhere Jen went, there were traces of the Frasers. Ardilla was completely taken over by them. She could tell from her parents' expressions that they were not pleased with her, that they thought she was being childish and spiteful, and that they wished she could be normal and happy like the other children. They all spent the day playing together with no quarrels at all while Jen hovered around them like an unhappy shadow, trying to get away, but having nowhere to escape to.

She was amazed that the day could be so beautiful when she felt so terrible. It seemed quite wrong that it should be bright and sunny outside and so dark and stormy inside her head. The waves lapped peacefully at the rocks, the leaves of the trees rustled and shimmered, little white clouds hovered on the horizon. The world went calmly on from morning through noon to late afternoon, as it did every day, while Jen struggled with her anger and unhappiness.

"What's the matter with you?" her mother asked her rather sharply, meeting her on the stairs towards the end of the day. "Are you still feeling sick?"

"I don't know," Jen said, longing to confide in her, but afraid of her impatience.

Shouts came from outside, where Mr Fraser was playing cricket with the other children. Jen's mother glanced towards the window. "You should be out there with the others."

"They don't want me," Jen replied.

"I'm sure they do! Perhaps you could make more of an effort to join in. Sally's such a nice girl. You two could be really good friends if you gave her a chance."

Sally's such a nice girl! Much nicer than you! That was how Jen heard it. It seemed to be the general opinion. Stuff them all, she thought furiously, and went on up the stairs to the attic rooms without saying any more to her mother.

The bedroom was no haven, however. It was too full of Sally's things for that. Jen looked at Sally's suitcase under the bed and thought with contempt about the stolen earrings hidden inside it. No one cares that she's a thief, she thought. I bet Dad hasn't done a thing about it. They forgive her anything because she's pretty and she acts cute. That's the only thing that matters to them. I don't play games like she does and so no one likes me! But at least I'm not dishonest.

Slightly comforted by this thought, she went to the window and watched the cricket game below. Her mother had joined the group and Mr Fraser was showing her how to hold the bat. He's got his arms round her! Jen was horrified. And she's laughing! Damn him, damn him! Why did he ever come here!

Beyond the paddock she could see the rocks of the little island tinged by the setting sun. Silhouetted black against the pale orange sky was a bird. She was sure it was her cormorant. Sitting there on its own, it looked as mournful as she felt. It rose with its harsh cry, flew clumsily for a few metres and then plunged into the water.

Once again Jen was drawn back into the old fantasies of childhood. The cormorant was a sign. It was telling her to do something. She let herself surrender to the mysteries of inner voices and hidden commands. She listened inwardly to the secret world of Ardilla, as she used to with Lisa and Tom and Richy when they played their complex and curious games. The other three had all abandoned the games and only she was left. They had not performed any of the rituals. They had forgotten their totem animals. No wonder the house was turning against her, no wonder its magic was lost.

She remembered the urgency of her dreams and her earlier decision to go on the roof. If no one else does the rituals I must do them myself, she thought. I'll go now while there's no one around.

With a new sense of purpose, she climbed out of the window and over the roof. In the valley between the gables she could still hear the others shouting and laughing, but she was isolated and completely alone. She thought no one had been here since last year, but half hidden under one of the slates was a bubblegum wrapper. It was new, it hadn't even been rained on. Someone had been up here recently.

As if numbed, Jen drew the sharkskin package from its hiding place. It had been shoved away carelessly, she could see at once, not carefully wrapped up as it had been at the end of the previous summer. She did not need to undo it; it fell open and the treasures rolled out. The crab's claw was broken, the black feather damaged by water. The fish skeleton stank, leaving a rotten smell over everything else.

The objects looked pathetic, spoiled. They had no power at all. Worse, the papers had been scrawled and scribbled over with some waxy red substance. Holding them to her nose, Jen smelled the faint smell of Sally's lipstick.

The others had been up on the roof, last night or early this morning, while she had been asleep. The Frasers had been shown the secret things of the Club and had destroyed them. She could not do the rituals and placate the totems. These objects had no power at all.

She had come here, to the heart of Ardilla, meaning to renew the rituals and reclaim her house, but now she was seized by self-contempt, as well as rage. How babyish it all seemed, and how unreal. Sally appeared unbelievably sophisticated in comparison. No wonder Tom had looked embarrassed and self-conscious about the Club. They had all grown out of it. It was all over. And she had been the last to realise it. What an idiot! She took the emblems and ground them beneath her feet. She tore the papers to shreds and shoved them in the gutter. Her eyes were starting to water, and that made her even angrier with herself. Crying like a baby over old and broken toys. But once they'd started, the tears wouldn't stop. Jen crouched on the roof of Ardilla and cried as if her world had come to an end.

9

I am filled with fear. There is no hope for me. There is no hope for my magic place. The emblems I put my trust in have been destroyed. The totems have lost their power. But when I go one more time down the steps that lead to the cellar below Ardilla I am not alone. A child comes with me. The child that will lead me past the bird. The child goes first down the steps and I follow. The child is brave. It walks down the steps without faltering, through the broken bones and claws. But when we reach the bottom it stops and turns back to me. It does not like the bird. Its eyes seek mine, huge and pleading.

I give the child to the bird, and it seizes it in its huge beak. The child screams to me, but I ignore it. It does not matter to me. The bird and the child disappear and I go past, into the rooms of beauty and grace that lie below Ardilla.

And the music plays. It has been playing all the time. It is the music that leads me. I follow it through rooms of incredible richness and splendour, marvelling that I never knew all this lay below Ardilla. I must find the flute player and make the music my own. Then my place will be safe forever.

So it's not all finished, Jen thought the following morning when she awoke from this dream. Everyone thinks the Club is over, but there's still something to be completed.

When she went downstairs, she stepped on something sharp. It crumbled beneath her foot, but not without piercing the skin. It was part of a crab's claw. She bent down and brushed the broken pieces away. A tiny splinter of shell had gone right into her foot and she could not get it out. While she was crouched there, her mother came past.

"What are you doing there?"

"I've got something in my foot," Jen replied.

"Let me have a look," her mother said.

"Don't worry about it," Jen said, straightening up, wanting her mother to worry about it, wanting her mother to make everything come right again.

But Mrs Gilroy took her at her word and walked on past her into the kitchen. "You can come and give me a hand," she called over her shoulder to Jen. "We'd better do something to get ready for this party tonight."

The Gilroys' wedding anniversary fell in the summer holidays, and it was a tradition to hold a party at Ardilla. Jen waited for the familiar surge of excitement, for party nights at Ardilla had always been times of special magic, but she felt only unease mingled with anger at her betrayal by the others.

When she entered the kitchen, she found them getting ready to go out with Mr Fraser. She looked at them coldly. No one said anything. Were their eyes mocking her? Did they know she knew what they had done? She had to confront them with it, but now was not the time— not with the adults in the kitchen, bustling about, busy and excited, making arrangements for the evening ahead.

"Joe's going to do the shopping for us," her mother explained. "But I don't suppose you want to go too, do you?"

"Not really," Jen replied. Mark made a face at her behind his father's back. She ignored him. She fiddled with the cutlery on the table. She couldn't wait for them to go. She longed to have Ardilla to herself.

"Got to take Sally down to see her dream boy," Mr Fraser said. "She's been nagging me to go back all week." He grinned at his daughter as he made this last remark and ducked as she swiped playfully at his head. "And I'm going to pick up the booze for the party and the eats." He shook his head at Jen's mother. "Fifteen years married," he said. "Beats me how you did it. You deserve a medal. Still, I might have chalked up a bit longer if I'd been married to you!"

"Get away with you," Mrs Gilroy said, sounding quite pleased.

Jen looked up sharply, and caught sight of Sally's face. The playfulness had been wiped from it. Sally stood as if stricken with grief, just as she had appeared on her first night at Ardilla, when Jen had watched her from behind the paddock wall.

"You look tired, Sally," Mrs Gilroy said. "Didn't you sleep well?"

"Nicky had another bad dream," Sally said.

"Oh, Nicky!" Mrs Gilroy bent over the little boy. "Tell Auntie Di about it!"

He looked seriously up at her. "That girl gave Nicky to the bad birdie!"

"Jen did?"

He nodded. "Naughty girl!"

"It's not my fault," Jen said when everyone stared at her. "I can't help what he dreams!"

"Out of the mouths of babes," Mr Fraser said, looking

86

at the ceiling.

Jen reached down and scratched at her foot. She felt the tiny piece of crab shell come out under her fingers.

"Come on, Dad," Sally said abruptly. "For heaven's sake let's get going."

She walked past Jen as though she wasn't there, and the others followed her.

"See you later," Richy muttered to her as he went past. She gave him an angry look. He hadn't protected the emblems. He'd let the others destroy them. It was no good being friendly now.

The avocado-green Mercedes disappeared down the driveway. Jen watched it from the veranda, relieved and delighted that the Frasers would be away for the whole day.

Calm descended on Ardilla. The day was perfect, sunny but not too hot. A breeze off the sea kept the house and garden cool, and the air was clear and crisp. Everything looked brighter than usual. All the colours were deeper and more intense. The simplest of things— the smell of lavender, the sparkling blue of the sea, the sight of her own tanned arm against the white sand— made Jen nearly delirious with a feeling that was too sharp to be happiness, too rich to be grief. It was as though the Frasers had disappeared off the face of the earth. She could almost believe her place had been restored to her.

After lunch, when it was too bright to go outside, she played the flute for a little while in the dining-room. There was no other sound inside her head, just Bach's glorious healing music. And when she had finished, there was no other ghostly music echoing hers and haunting her.

If only it could stay like this for ever, Jen thought. If only my life could stop here.

But little by little the day drew to a close. The time for the party approached. The Frasers would be back soon. The confrontation with the others was drawing near. Jen could feel them getting closer. Her head began to ache again, and a feeling of menace came over her.

She was in the kitchen, helping her father sort out and dust the drinking glasses, when her mother came in, looking anxious.

"No sign of them," Mrs Gilroy said. "They're awfully late. Joe said they'd be back at four and it's after six! People will be arriving at seven! We've got nothing ready!"

"You know Joe," Mr Gilroy said, rather sourly. "He's not the most reliable guy on earth."

"I hope they haven't had an accident!"

"More likely to have stopped off for a drink!"

"Not when he's driving, surely?"

Mum! Jen almost swore in exasperation at her mother. Fancy not realising that Mr Fraser was perfectly capable of drinking and driving. For a moment she felt she was the shrewd and sensible parent and her mother a hopelessly naive child.

She dusted out the last few Vegemite jars, and put them on the table.

"What'll I do now, Mum?"

Mrs Gilroy did not answer her. She was listening intently. "Oh, I think I can hear them now," she said with a sigh of relief.

Jen went to the kitchen door and looked round the side of the house, wondering if they were having a shot at the record.

The Mercedes was not racing down the driveway, braking in a shower of gravel and dust. It came very slowly and stopped very sedately.

One wing was smashed in, the paintwork scraped all along the side, the headlight broken.

Sally stepped out of the car and without looking at her father walked away from the house towards the beach.

"Oh my God, they have had an accident!" Mrs Gilroy pushed past Jen and ran to the car.

Mr Fraser got out, looking thoroughly fed up. "Nothing to worry about, Di," he said. "Just a little prang. No one's hurt."

"We were starting to get a bit concerned!"

"Well, we're back now. Come on kids, get moving and bring the stuff in."

Mr Fraser slung a crate of beer under one arm and picked up two bags of groceries. He walked away from the car as if it was nothing to do with him and came through the kitchen door without looking at Jen. Mrs Gilroy followed him into the house.

"What happened?" Jen grabbed Lisa's arm as she went past, holding a watermelon.

"Watch out, you'll make me drop it," Lisa exclaimed.

"Give it to me, I'll carry it for you. But tell me what happened!" Jen was both elated and shocked by the damaged car. She wondered if her ill-wishing had had something to do with it. She hoped it had.

"Mr Fraser drove into a post!" Lisa gave the melon to Jen, and pushed her hair away from her eyes.

"Were you going really fast?"

"I don't want to talk about it here. I'll tell you in a minute. Something bad happened."

"What?" Jen pursued the others into the kitchen and

put the watermelon down on the table.

No one said anything as they put down the shopping bags. The kitchen was in chaos; all the adults were in there, grabbing the food and drink as it arrived and frantically making preparations for the party. Nicky was clinging to his father's legs and whining.

"I'm hungry, Daddy!"

"For God's sake," Mr Fraser said, impatiently. "Where on earth is Sally? Mark, can you take Nicky outside for a couple of minutes while I get organised? Try and find your sister and tell her to come and help."

"Come on, Nicky!" Mark said, resigned, and took his little brother by the hand. As if responding to a signal, the others followed him. Jen went after them, burning with curiosity.

"What happened?" she said again when they were outside.

"You'll be really thrilled," Mark said to her spitefully. His face was very pale, and he was trembling a little. "It's just what you wanted. In fact, I reckon it's all your fault!"

She didn't answer. She looked from one to the other, wondering if anyone was going to tell her.

Richy said, "You can't blame her, she wasn't even there."

Mark needed to talk about it. "We weren't even going very fast. Dad was in a terrible temper with Sally and he wasn't looking where he was going. I hate it when he gets in rages. I've always hated it. You don't know what it's like. He's usually nice when there are other people around."

"He was terribly angry," Lisa agreed with a little nervous laugh.

"But why was he so angry?" Jen persisted.

Nicky began to cry. "I'm hungry, Mark!"

Mark gave Richy a nudge. "You tell her," he said. "I'm going to get Sally. Come on, Nicky."

"I suppose you'll know sooner or later," Richy said to Jen. "It was all to do with the earrings."

"The ones you said she'd nicked," Lisa put in.

"She did nick them!"

"Yeah, we know! Sally was talking to that boy she really likes outside Mrs Weston's shop, and Mrs Weston came out. She remembered her."

Jen could guess what was coming next. She went hot and cold all over just thinking about it.

"We were all hanging around waiting for Sally," Richy went on. "So we heard every word. It was so embarrassing!"

"Specially it being Mrs Weston," Tom put in. "She's always been so nice to us."

Lisa took over. "Mrs Weston said Sally had pinched some earrings from the shop last time she was there. Well, Sally started denying it, of course, and then Mr Fraser showed up. Mrs Weston was being really nice about it, said she didn't want to involve the police or anything, since she knew us, but she didn't think kids should get away with that sort of thing . . ."

"First of all Mr Fraser got angry at Mrs Weston," Tom said, sounding indignant, "but Sally was actually wearing the earrings, so then he was furious with her. He made her take the earrings off and give them back. They had this huge row in front of everyone . . ."

"Especially the boy," Lisa groaned. "That was the worst bit! I don't understand why she wore them. She must be crazy!"

"Either she thought she was completely safe," Tom

said thoughtfully, "or she wanted to be caught!"

"Anyway," Richy wanted to get on with the story, "when we got in the car Mr Fraser wasn't looking where he was going and he drove straight into a post. And then he was really mad!"

"Geez!" Jen said. She couldn't think of anything else to say. She was confused by her own reaction. She had wanted Sally's theft of the earrings to be discovered; she didn't think people ought to be allowed to get away with stealing either; but she was surprised at how sorry she felt for Sally. To be accused in public! And talking to the boy she really liked! Just the thought of something like that happening to her made her feel sick.

Before any of them could say anything else, the kitchen door opened and Mrs Gilroy called, "Jen, Lisa! We need some help in here please."

"We'll wait for Mark," Richy said. "Be in in a minute."

Jen wondered how much the adults knew. They were too busy to discuss it. Their guests would be arriving any minute. No one mentioned the earrings as they chopped up salad and fruit, though when the men went outside to get the fire started for the barbecue, they all had a look at the dented Mercedes and commiserated with Mr Fraser.

Mrs Gilroy and Mrs Melville were also outside, setting up the trestle tables and putting out plates and glasses, when Sally came back into the kitchen with Nicky. She did not look at Jen. Her face was calm and impassive. She made scrambled egg for her brother and sat him at the table to eat it. Jen went on slicing tomatoes in silence.

Lisa, who was grating carrots, was more daring. "Hey,

Sally! Why on earth did you wear the earrings today?"

"Mind your own business," Sally said. "You don't know anything about it."

Lisa held her tongue, grated carrot and then hummed a little tune to herself.

The three boys came into the kitchen.

"Gee, I'm starving!" Richy scooped a handful of grated carrot out of the bowl and crammed it into his mouth. "It's going to be hours before the meat's cooked." He took a couple of slices of tomato.

Jen threatened him with the knife. "You'll get your fingers cut off!"

Tom broke off a piece of french bread and gave it to Mark. "We'd better all have something to eat now."

"I'm not hungry," Mark said, putting the bread down on the table.

Richy looked from him to Sally and back again. "Cheer up!" he said, in an effort to lighten the atmosphere. "It's party night! It's full moon! Magical things happen at Ardilla on party night!"

"In your dreams!" Sally said spitefully.

"We usually have fun!" Richy persisted. "What'll we do tonight to make it special?" he said to Jen.

"Play infantile games on the roof, I suppose," Sally sneered. She stared at Jen challengingly.

There was an awkward silence. Jen said, "I've been up there. I know you all wrecked everything. You shouldn't have done it." She looked away from Sally to Tom.

"It was getting a bit childish," he mumbled, his face scarlet.

"It was our secret," she said. "You shouldn't have shown Sally and Mark."

Sally looked straight at Jen. "You don't own this

house, you know!" she said aggressively. "It's not your place. We've got just as much right to be here as you. We can go up on the roof if we want to."

"Well, sure," Tom put in, trying to make peace between the two girls.

Richy backed him up. "We could all do the Club together."

"Ha! Ha!" Sally scoffed. "You and your stupid club. All are id! All are mad, more like!"

Outside a gust of wind struck a few notes from the wind chimes. The sound was mysterious, almost sinister. Jen had a sudden unpleasant impression of the house distorting itself again. The kitchen floor sloped upwards and the walls began to close in. Inside her head something echoed, unrelenting. Patterns moved in front of her eyes. The totems were taking shape before her. Richy put out his hand to ruffle Nicky's hair and it looked like a huge crab's claw. Tom's eyes bulged out and his mouth opened, fishlike. Lisa's head bobbed, and beneath her firm, fair skin Jen saw the skull of a bird.

"Don't," she said warningly to Sally. "Don't say anything else." It came out differently from how she had meant it. Her voice sounded harsh and angry, as though another creature was speaking through her.

"Geez, you're pathetic," Sally sneered.

Dammit! Jen thought. She's the one who should be ashamed of herself, and she's standing there attacking me! She looked back as though from a huge distance at the golden day, dimly aware that it was the last day of childhood.

"Come on," Richy pleaded. "Don't let's spend the party night quarrelling! It's such a waste."

"What happens on party night?" Mark asked, but

94

before Richy could answer, there was a shout from outside. "Come here, kids, we need a hand with the wood!"

"Coming!" Tom shouted back, and he and Richy left the kitchen. Lisa jumped up quickly and followed them.

Sally gave Nicky the last spoonful of scrambled egg and wiped his face with his bib. "I suppose I'd better give him a bath. What a holiday! Perhaps I will go home."

After a few moments' silence, Jen said, "Go home?"

"Dad says I can go home if I want to," Sally replied coolly.

"That's not quite what Dad said," Mark burst out. "He said he'd send you home if you didn't behave yourself."

"Drop dead!" Sally snapped at him. "It's nothing to do with you."

Mark made a face at his sister and ran outside after the others.

"Do you want to go home?" Jen asked. It occurred to her suddenly that Sally was probably missing her mother.

"You'd love it, wouldn't you?" Jen's sympathy was lost on Sally. "Then you'd have your precious place all to yourself again. You wouldn't be jealous of me all the time!"

"I'm not jealous of you," Jen replied, amazed.

"Everyone thinks you are. I heard your mum tell Dad."

Jen hated the idea that her mother was discussing her with Mr Fraser. "Who'd be jealous of you! You're a thief!"

"Aw, shut up," Sally snarled. "You don't know anything about anything. You're just a silly little kid who thinks she's great because she can play a few tunes on a flute."

"I wish you would go home," Jen couldn't help

responding.

"I'd love to go home! But I'm going to stay because you don't want me to. Ready, Nicky? I'm going to put you to bed so I can have some fun."

Nicky was protesting that he didn't want to go to bed when the other four came back into the kitchen, giggling and shoving each other.

"Guess what?" Richy said to Jen. "Mark wants to do the Club."

"It's all wrecked," Jen said. "It's finished." But something echoed in her head and she knew it was not finished, not yet.

"We can do something, though," Richy insisted. "We can play something. Something . . . spooky!"

"Have a challenge!" Tom suggested, his normally placid face starting to light up with excitement. "Some kind of test!"

"That's the sort of thing we do on party night," Richy told Mark. "Something really dangerous and daring!"

"The grown-ups never notice because they're all having fun," Lisa added. "Drinking and dancing and so on."

"We stay up all night, nearly," Tom said. "And no one tells us to go to bed or anything."

"Big deal!" Sally sneered.

Tom stopped suddenly, and some of the excitement went out of his face.

Seeing him put down like that made Jen mad. "We'll challenge you!" she said boldly to Sally. "We'll make a test for you. And if you lose it, you've got to go home."

"Don't involve me," Sally said. "I'm not interested."

"We're going to steal something from you," Jen said, aware that the eyes of the others were all on her, aware

96

that she had somehow taken the leadership back from Sally. "Something that you really like. Then you'll know what it means to lose things."

Sally replied sharply, "I know that . . .!"

Sadness pressed down on Jen, making her flinch from it. She wanted to get rid of the sadness, get rid of Sally, get rid of the pain of having to feel sorry for someone she would rather hate.

"Come on, Sal," Mark begged his sister. "It'll be fun!"

"We dare you," Jen said.

Sally looked from Jen to Mark and back again. There was a moment when excitement flared between the two girls.

Sally's eyes began to burn. "You can't all be against me," she said. "I need someone on my side."

You had everyone against me, Jen thought, but aloud she said, "Mark can be with you."

"And Richy," Mark said swiftly, putting his arm over his friend's shoulder.

"OK," Richy said good-naturedly. "But what's the challenge going to be?"

Nicky had grasped something of what was going on, and he was leaning over the table, banging his spoon on it. "Want to play too!" he demanded.

"You're going to bed, mate," Sally said, picking him up.

He wriggled out of her arms and on to the floor. "No carry me!" he said, fiercely. "Not a baby. Want to play!"

"I know you're not a baby," Sally said patiently, her face softening.

Jen noticed the softening, felt the sadness enveloping her, wanted to fight it, wanted to feel again the rightness of hating Sally, and heard herself say, as though someone else was speaking through her, "Nicky can play! Nicky can be what we steal!"

10

They stared at her in silence for a few moments.

"It'd be better to steal something that doesn't yell!" Mark said.

"Nicky won't yell," Jen replied, "will you, Nicky? You want to play, don't you?"

"Yes, want to play," he agreed firmly.

"We'll steal Nicky and hide him where you can't find him. And if you haven't found him by sunrise tomorrow, you have to go home."

"OK," Sally said. Then she added mockingly, "It's not much of a test. You'll never win. I'm the only one Nicky likes, so you're not going to get him away from me."

"That's not true!" Lisa said. "Nicky likes Tom. And me!" She knelt down in front of the little boy. "Do you want me to give you a piggyback, Nicky?"

He nodded eagerly and held out his arms. Lisa turned round, still crouching, so he could climb on her back.

"Hold tight!" she shouted. "Going for a horsey ride! You don't want to stay with Sally! Sally wants to put you to bed. You're going to come and play all night with us!"

She ran outside, Nicky squealing with excitement and delight. The others tore after her.

Lisa ran as far as the paddock wall before Mark caught up with her. He grabbed his brother by the legs and tried to pull him off Lisa's back. Lisa twisted round and hung on to Nicky's arms as hard as she could. Nicky, who was being pulled in half between them, bit his lip and tried not to cry.

"Let go of him!" Sally raced up. "He's not some sort of object! You can't treat him like that! The whole thing's off if you're going to hurt him."

"Sorry." Lisa stood back, ashamed. "It was Mark's fault. He grabbed him!"

"He's my brother! I can do that!"

"It's not fair if you can and we can't," Lisa protested.

"We'd better make a rule—no force," Tom said, coming up behind them. "Nicky's got to choose really. It's whoever's nicest to him."

"You want to read stories?" Richy suggested to Nicky.

"Yes!" Nicky said.

"I'll read you one," Lisa said promptly, and took Nicky by the hand.

"Not fair!" Richy groaned. "It was my idea!"

They squabbled about it briefly, and then began to trail back towards the house.

Jen stood watching for a few moments before following them. The sun was setting, and Ardilla had taken on its golden evening glow. A car came down the driveway, the sun flashing on its windscreen as it emerged from under the pines. The five adults were all outside. Her father and Mr Melville, wearing brightly coloured aprons, were standing by the barbecue. Mrs Melville was arranging bowls of salad on the trestle table. Mr Fraser was pouring a drink. He handed it to Jen's mother, who was sitting on one of the banana chairs under the pergola. They clinked their glasses together, and Mr Fraser said something that made Mrs Gilroy laugh.

Jen heard shouts of greeting as the first guests got out of their car and crossed the grass. She did not want to go down and meet them, hear them exclaiming how much she'd grown since last year, and answer their dumb questions about school. Instead she ran after the others, catching up with them as they were about to go back inside the house.

"How about hide-and-seek?" she said. "Nicky, do you want to play hide-and-seek?"

"Yes, yes!" he begged, jumping up and down with excitement.

The sun set and the light faded. The outside lamps and citronella candles kept the barbecue area bright, but the rest of the house was in darkness. The adults sat outside with their food and drinks. The house became the children's.

The warmth and the heaviness of the summer night sent them slightly mad. The air was thick with the fragrance of flowers, covering the darker smell of beach and tea-tree. Crickets chirped and then stopped suddenly, the silence more piercing than the noise. Doors and steps that had been soundless now creaked with menace. A full moon rose and birds were confused by its brightness, taking it for the dawn and singing a phrase before they realised their mistake and slept again.

And the other Ardilla, the one that had always existed and had lain there for years waiting to be unlocked, began to emerge. The house with its strange inner rooms was coming alive.

The children discovered hiding places they had not known were there. They crouched, hidden, as if turned to stone, for what seemed to them to be a lifetime.

Time changed. The night became endless. It stretched

out before them like eternity. Nothing else would ever happen. They would go on forever, playing hide-and-seek at Ardilla. They no longer knew—it no longer mattered—who was hiding and who was seeking. They hid . . . and when no one discovered them, they crept out and went on the long, silent hunt through the dark house, coming upon each other with muffled shrieks and shudders of wild laughter.

First Nicky was with Jen, hiding under the bed in her parents' room, but the dust made him cough and Mark found them there. Nicky could slip out of the cramped space more easily than Jen, and by the time she had wriggled clear she found she had lost him in the dark.

Mark's carried him off somewhere, she thought to herself. She heard a creak above her head as though someone was tiptoeing through the attic rooms. She went quietly to the stairs and listened.

The creak came again. Someone was up there. She climbed the first two stairs and then stopped, flattening herself against the wall.

A light went on in the passage and she heard the toilet flush. Then she heard Mr Fraser's voice, from the direction of his bedroom. "Just came in to get some more smokes!"

He was speaking to someone she could not see, but his voice was warm and friendly.

Then there was a silence, but she had the idea that whoever was there had not gone away.

She was right, for a few seconds later she heard her mother say, briskly, "Come along, Joe, we must get back to the others."

"No hurry," Mr Fraser said.

Jen did not dare look. She did not know what she

feared to see, she just knew she was terrified of seeing it. She froze against the wall. Her heart was beating painfully. She ran her hand over the narrow stair rail. It felt different. There was something on it, some sort of carving. She tried to discern what it was with her fingertips.

Footsteps went away from her and she heard the screen door from the kitchen slam. Her mother and Mr Fraser had gone outside.

She was about to go down the stairs again when something touched her on the neck. She couldn't help screaming. Then there was a burst of giggles.

"Caught ya!" Tom hissed in her ear.

"Are you it?"

"I got tired of hiding. No one came to find me. So I thought I'd see who I could find."

"Who's got Nicky?"

"I don't know. I haven't seen him."

"Tom," Jen said, taking his hand and guiding it to the stair rail. "Feel this. Doesn't it feel like it's got something carved in it?"

"Feels the same as usual to me. Just as splintery as ever!"

But it had not felt splintery to her. It had felt smooth, except for the carving.

"I'm going to put the light on for a minute," she said.

The brightness made them both blink. Tom put his hand to his mouth and bit at his palm. "I did get a splinter," he complained.

The rail was its normal rough, uncarved self. But when Jen put her hand down again she could feel the other rail. It was emerging from the ordinary everyday one as if it was growing out of it. She could feel the shapes coming through. A crab's claw, a bird's beak.

She put both hands up to her mouth.

"Did you get a splinter too?" Tom said. "I can't get mine out."

"Let's go find the others," Jen said. She wanted to get outside. Her head felt strange, not exactly aching, but pulsating. She could feel the house changing around her. The other Ardilla, the secret Ardilla of her dreams, was taking shape around her.

Tom put up his hand and clicked the light switch off. The darkness was total, making him snort in fright. Jen heard a creak as he crossed the passage, but she could not see him.

She found it hard to move. She feared she would take one step and find herself in the other Ardilla, unable to get out of it. She wanted to reach it, she wanted to explore its beauty and strangeness, but it also filled her with awe and terror.

It's going too far, she thought rapidly. It's all getting out of hand. I must put a stop to it. I must stop hearing voices and having dreams.

Then the door of the kitchen swung open and light filled the passage. She could hear the other children laughing and talking. The way ahead was quite clear and simple. She walked down the passage and into the kitchen.

"Food break!" Richy sang out, cheerfully. His cheeks were flushed and his eyes bright. He was sitting on the table with his feet on a chair. Mr Fraser was at the fridge, taking out ice cream.

"You've all been terrific babysitters," he said, turning round and giving them a huge smile. "Nicky's had the time of his life, haven't you, mate? Ice cream all round as a reward! And then off to bed with you, old son!"

"We want to play some more games with him," Lisa said. "We're going to teach him how to play Fish!" She dropped a kiss on the top of Nicky's head. "He's rather cute, isn't he? I wish we had a little brother!"

Mr Fraser served ice cream to the children and then took the tub outside. As he left the kitchen Jen's mother came in. They made a bit of a performance about nearly crashing into each other in the doorway.

"Oh, Joe, you've got the ice cream! I'll just get the fruit salad!" Mrs Gilroy exclaimed. She took the huge glass bowl from the fridge and swung through the door as Mr Fraser held it open for her, giving him a laughing glance of thanks as she passed him.

"Come outside if you want fruit salad, kids," she called back into the kitchen.

Jen followed her out. The screen door swung back, nearly hitting her in the face, as Mr Fraser let go of it to pursue her mother. She stood in the shadow of the house and watched them walk, laughing and joking, across to the table. Then she was aware of another figure standing watching just as she was, but on the opposite side of the barbecue area, as if on the third point of a triangle. It was her father, alone, drink in hand, watching her mother and Mr Fraser. The fear of seeing things she did not want to see came back to her. She looked at him, longing for him to move, to speak, to laugh, anything to break the fixed quality of his stare. All the others were enjoying themselves hugely. Only her father was on the outside, sad and alone. She felt sorry for him—and tremendously impatient. She wanted him to snap out of his isolation, physically to drag her mother away from Mr Fraser.

He's pathetic, she thought, at the same time feeling an aching pity for him. Why doesn't he try to look as though he's having fun!

Then Mr Melville went over, refilled her father's glass, and started talking to him. They seemed to be having quite an animated conversation. But her mother still stayed close to Mr Fraser.

Jen could hear the other children shrieking over the game of cards. She did not want to be alone any more. She was afraid of what might happen to her. She was afraid she would go on seeing and feeling things that weren't really there. The company of the others kept the other Ardilla at bay. It could not emerge completely and trap her if she stayed with them. She went back into the house.

Nicky had taken a liking to Lisa and was sitting on her knee. By the time they had played another couple of games of Fish he was nearly asleep, his thumb in his mouth, his eyelids drooping.

"You're heavy," Lisa told him. "A heavy little dumpling!"

He smiled and yawned, snuggling into her. She grinned with delight.

"I'd better put him to bed," Sally said, standing up. What had happened to her while they were playing hide-and-seek, Jen wondered. She looked younger and less sophisticated, and the hurt, cold look had gone from her face.

"Aren't we going to play any more?" Richy said. "It was fun!"

"It's more fun when we all play together," Tom said gruffly, looking at Jen.

"It was ace," Mark announced. "This is an ace house!

106

It's the best holiday I've ever had. Apart from pranging the Merc. That was a bit of a downer!"

"Can I put him to bed?" Lisa asked, standing up and hoisting Nicky on to her hip.

"Not if you're going to steal him away!" Sally replied.

"Of course I'm not! Actually, I'd forgotten the challenge! I thought we were all just having fun playing games with him!"

"Well, OK. Nicky, do you want Lisa to put you to bed?"

Nicky smiled, too tired to answer, and buried his head in Lisa's shoulder. She went pink with pleasure.

"Is the challenge over?" Richy said.

Tom looked at Jen. "Is it?"

She shrugged. "Up to everyone."

They all looked at each other and laughed.

Richy said, not giving Sally time to speak, "So what'll we do now? It's too early to go to bed."

"What's the latest you ever went to bed?" Mark asked him.

"I stayed up all night once. When we went to Kangaroo Island."

"I once went to bed at four o'clock in the morning. I stayed at my friend's place and we watched horror movies and then we told ghost stories!"

"Let's tell ghost stories now!" Richy said eagerly.

"Sal knows some horrors!" Mark said in a creepy voice. "You'll never get to sleep!"

The noise of the party faded a little behind them as the children left the kitchen. Moonlight shone through the windows, making the rooms ghostly and strange. Jen walked warily, staying close to the others. The moonlight fell on the patch of floor where in the other Ardilla steps led down to the cellar. She skirted it, not daring to walk through it. The house was quiet. It was waiting for her. As they reached the attic stairs, she looked back. For a moment she saw the steps, saw them leading down, nearly ran to them. She clung to the stair rail, felt the carvings again under her fingers, let go of it as though it was red hot.

"Calm down," Tom said. "If you're that jumpy now, what'll you be like after a few ghost stories?"

"You're not scared of ghosts, are you?" Mark said in scorn.

You don't know anything, Jen thought. You wouldn't notice if the whole house was haunted! Then she shivered. For Ardilla was haunted—but not in a way that anyone else would ever suspect. She was the only one who knew, and only she was going to . . .

Going to what? She caught herself in time. She was not going to do anything. She was going to stay close to the others. She was not going to let herself get caught up in any more fantasies. The relief she felt at this decision made her quite sleepy. I could just go to sleep, forget all about the strange things that have been happening, and in the morning everything will be OK, she thought. She walked up the stairs without touching the rails.

Something was crunching under her feet. Gritting her teeth and clenching her fists, she walked through it.

Lisa caught up with them as they settled themselves down on the vinyl-covered floor of Neutral Ground.

"Nicky went to sleep as soon as he lay down!" she said, amazed. "He's so cute!"

"He's not always cute," Mark replied. "You should try living with him all the time!"

"Oh, he's pretty good," Sally added quickly. "Particularly when you think of all he's gone through."

"You must miss your dad when you're in Melbourne," Lisa said sympathetically.

"What do you reckon?" Sally retorted defensively.

Geez, she's prickly! Jen thought. It's so easy to get on the wrong side of her. Hearing Sally snap at Lisa riled her. She really needs to be taught a lesson, Jen thought. I wish we'd won the challenge. I'm sure we could have got Nicky away, specially since he likes Lisa so much.

She remembered that neither she nor Sally had agreed that the challenge was over. So it needn't be over, she told herself. We could still get Nicky before morning.

But the thought of walking down the stairs again, and crossing the patch where the steps led down to the cellar, filled her with apprehension. I suppose it's best not to wake him up, she reasoned. And anyway, you can't really take a little kid out in the middle of the night. I'm much too sleepy too! Sitting in the dark on the floor of Neutral Ground, she found she couldn't stop yawning.

"And then," Sally was half way through her first story, "he put the car radio on and he heard a police message and they said . . ."

"Oh, I've heard this one," Richy said. "But the version I heard happened in Broken Hill, not West Wyalong, and it was a guy and his girlfriend, not a man and his son."

"And the police tell him not to look back?"

"That's right! But she looks back—"

"And the maniac's banging the head on the roof of the car!"

"Yeah!"

"Ugh!" Lisa said. "Actually, I've heard it too!"

"It's kind of a strange story," Tom said. "I mean, if you think about it, it's not really logical. It doesn't make sense."

Jen yawned again. She was about to say she agreed with Tom, it didn't make sense, not in any of the versions she'd heard, and it wasn't even scary, just gross, but suddenly talking seemed like too much effort. She shifted around until she could lie down, and pillowed her head on her arms.

"Horror stories aren't meant to make sense," Sally said cheerfully. "They're just meant to scare the hell out of you! Have you heard this one? A woman was walking home from work one night and she saw a stray dog outside her house . . ."

"Oh, this is bad!" Mark said. "Don't tell this one, Sal!"

"Well, if you want to wimp out . . ."

The others begged her to tell it. Jen shut her eyes. Then she opened them again. It was as dark with them open as with them shut, but for a moment she thought she saw patterns in the darkness—the shape of a feather, the outline of a claw.

The house was awakening.

In the distance she could hear the faint music from the party, quieter now and more dreamy, and behind it she could hear something else.

Surely someone was playing her flute.

Sally's voice went on, but Jen hardly heard the story. She was drifting between waking and sleeping. The music called her, but she did not want to get up and follow it. Her limbs were heavy with apprehension. She knew that if she went down the stairs she would walk straight into the other Ardilla, she would meet the other flute player, and she would never get out. The sound of the flute, Sally's voice telling one story after another, the groans of the others, wove themselves into her dreams.

11

Jen drifted upwards through shallow sleep, and opened her eyes to the grey light of daybreak. She was lying on her back on her own bed, still in her clothes from the night before. Lisa was snoring lightly on the stretcher. Sally slept with the same air of neatness and competence with which she did everything else.

Jen had the tired, wiped-out feeling that comes from a very late night and a lot of excitement, and she would have turned over and gone back to sleep, but she needed to go to the toilet badly, and she was hot and thirsty. More than that, there was something battering urgently at the door of her consciousness as though it was trying to give her important instructions.

She got quietly out of bed and crept down the stairs. When she came out of the bathroom, she noticed that the door to Mr Fraser's room was slightly open. From inside came subdued singing and chattering. Nicky was awake.

Nicky!

It was not yet sunrise.

She could take him away and hide him, and she would have won the challenge.

Sally would have to go home and Ardilla would be the same as it used to be.

She pushed the door open a little more and looked in.

Nicky was sitting up in the cot. He looked at her and then he looked past her and said clearly, "Birdie!"

Jen looked behind her. "What birdie?"

"Naughty birdie," Nicky said, frowning at it. "Naughty birdie get Nicky!"

"No one's going to get you," Jen said.

Mr Fraser turned and muttered in the bed.

Jen tiptoed across the room, her finger to her lips. "Sshh! Don't wake up your dad!"

"Don't wake Daddy!" he agreed.

"You want to come outside with me?" she whispered.

"OK!" He looked at her. "Get dressed first?"

"No, you don't have to get dressed. You're OK in your pyjamas."

They were bright blue with little white sailboats on them. Nicky's cheeks were still pink with sleep and his hair was damp. Jen helped him climb out of the cot and pulled him out of the room, closing the door quietly behind them.

"Breakfast?" Nicky asked hopefully as they hurried through the silent kitchen. The debris from the party was piled high on the worktops and in the sink.

"We don't want to wake anyone up," Jen muttered. She grabbed the biscuit container from the pantry and carried it outside. Opening it, she discovered three chocolate biscuits. She gave two to Nicky and started to eat one herself, but the taste nauseated her and she threw it on the ground.

Nicky chewed up his unusual breakfast without comment as Jen hurried him across the yard and into the paddock.

"Ow!" he exclaimed before they had gone more than a few steps. He stood on one leg, then the other. His face

112

started to crumple.

"Nicky," Jen said urgently. "You remember the game we played last night? You promised you wouldn't cry. This is still part of the game. You mustn't cry!"

"Prickles," he explained, trying to hold back the tears.

"I'll carry you. I'll give you a piggyback!"

He liked that, but half way across the paddock he started to wriggle around until she nearly dropped him.

"Keep still! What's wrong?"

"Need a wee-wee!"

"Oh, geez! Wait till we get to the beach. If you wee down my back, you're dead!" Jen began to trot like a pony. Nicky laughed and clutched tight at her neck.

"Ouch! You're pulling my hair!"

His body was warm against her back, and he smelt rather nice. She felt a rush of affection for him. When they got to the beach she knelt down and he slid off her back on to the sand. He pulled down his pyjama pants and peed with great enthusiasm into the sea. Then he pointed out towards the island and shouted, "Look! Birdie!"

The tide was just past full and beginning to ebb. Rocks, sea and sand were different shades of grey. Jen could see the black shape of the cormorant in the water, between the shore and the island.

"What's it doing, Jen?" Nicky came and took her hand. He seemed apprehensive about something. She realised that it was the first time he had used her name.

"It's fishing for its breakfast," she replied.

"No, not fishing; dying," he said simply.

"Don't be silly," she said sharply. "It's not dying!"

He withdrew his hand, hurt. "You're silly."

"It's just fishing. It'll come up again soon."

113

But the cormorant did not come up. It rolled in the swell. It could get its head above water, but something was preventing it from flying up as it should have done.

"See," Nicky said. "It is dying. It's drowning!"

It can't be drowning, Jen thought, bewildered. It's a seabird. How can it drown?

But there was no doubt about it. It was drowning before her eyes.

Inside her head the urgent command mounted to a shriek. She shook with panic and confusion. Her bird was dying. She had to save it.

She pulled her jumper off over her head.

"Stay here!" she ordered Nicky, and ran into the sea.

The water was cold, and it deepened very quickly. She swam towards the bird as fast as she could, but she was surprised at how tired and heavy her arms and legs felt. When the bird saw her, its eyes rolled in fear, and it struggled harder to rise out of the water.

She reached it and took it in her arms. It pecked feebly at her hands. Remembering the lifesaving techniques she had been taught, she turned on her back and tried to hold its head up out of the water. It struggled, but weakly, so weakly that she thought at any moment it would cease struggling altogether.

She was only twenty metres or so out from shore, but swimming back took a long time. The ebbing tide and the offshore dawn wind combined to push her out to sea. She gritted her teeth and swam as strongly as she could. Eventually she tried for the bottom, found it, turned, and, holding the bird up in front of her, walked up on to the shore.

Nicky touched the bird's head wonderingly. "Is he dead?"

Jen dropped to her knees on the sand, and cradled the cormorant in her arms. It was floppy and feeble. It had lost the power that held it together, that enabled it to fly and fish and dive and swim. It made one last desperate lunge to rise out of her arms and then it fell back. Its head dropped to one side and the light went out of its eyes forever.

She turned it over, and saw the line hanging from its beak. She opened the beak carefully. The hook must have embedded itself in the bird's throat. The throat was almost closed up with pus. Her bird had swallowed the fishing line and choked to death on it.

"Stupid fools!" she swore at them all, at Mr Fraser and his family, and at Tom and Richy and Lisa who had joined sides with them. Her precious bird was dead. They had killed it.

Tears stung her eyes but she fought them back. She was not going to cry. She was going to get revenge. The totems demanded it. They had been forgotten, spurned, mocked—but now they were going to get their own back. They were going to prove they were not just part of a pathetic, childish game. They had not after all been destroyed on the roof. They had come alive and had found their ancient power. The real cormorant was dead, but the totem cormorant, the symbol, was alive, and demanding vengeance.

She laid the bird on the sand and stood up, looking round, trying to listen inside her head, trying to hear what it was telling her.

"Poor birdie," Nicky said, stroking its head gently. He looked up at Jen to see what she was going to do or say, but she stood completely silent, as if turned to stone, peering out to the island and scowling. He moved away, a little nervous of her, looking for something else to do, something to distract her with. His eyes fell on the boat, which had been left on the beach above the high water line.

"Jen!" he said. "You take Nicky out in the boat?"

When she did not reply he repeated it, more loudly. "Nicky want to go out in the boat!"

The sound inside her head was resolving itself at last into a voice. She listened to it intently.

Take me home, it was saying. *Take me home*.

She looked at the dead cormorant. She didn't want to leave it here where everyone else would see it. She looked across at the island.

Nicky pulled at her hand. "Jen, let's go out in the boat!"

"OK," she said quietly. That was what she would do. She would take the cormorant home to the island in the boat.

"Can we?" Nicky was astonished by her agreement. "Can we really?"

"Sure," she said. It all seemed quite clear to her now. She would take Nicky to the island and take the cormorant home.

There was one lifejacket in the bottom of the boat. The others, Jen knew, would be up in the house. Well, she didn't need one. She laid the dead cormorant gently on the plank seat and picked up the lifejacket.

"Here." She held it out to Nicky. "Put this on!"

He was jumping up and down with excitement. He had forgotten the dead bird. He struggled into the lifejacket and she fastened it in front for him. Then he ran to the stern and began to try to pull the boat into the water.

"Hang on," Jen said. "I'll lift it. You get up in front

and push."

It was hard, heavy work, but after five back-breaking minutes they had the boat afloat in the shallows. Holding firmly on to the rope, Jen lifted Nicky in. His pyjamas were already soaking wet, and he was shivering a little.

"Nicky, you're cold." She realised she was freezing too, her wet clothes clammy against her skin. For a moment common sense made a claim on her. She stared at the little boy, his lifejacket swamping him, his cheeks pale. "Perhaps we'd better go later. When it's a bit warmer, and the others are around."

"Not cold," he said firmly. "Want to go now!"

She took her wet T-shirt off and put her jumper on.

Take me home, the voice shrieked inside her head. And then it added, *Give me the child. Give me the child and I will be at peace.*

The boat pulled away from her as the ebb tide flowed more strongly out of the bay. She jumped in, floundering a little on the side. When she had the oars in her hands and began to row, she was surprised to see how far out they were already.

She had to row really hard to get to the island. The tide kept pulling the boat away and out into the open bay beyond. Her arms were aching and her hands tired by the time she managed to get the bow of the boat up against the rocks.

"Jump off," she said to Nicky.

He sat and clung to the side of the boat.

"Don't you want to get off?" she asked. "I thought you wanted to explore the island."

"Nicky want to go home," he said. The distance from land, the depth of the sea were alarming him. "Nicky want Sally!"

Behind him Jen could see Ardilla. She could see someone on the veranda. Then she heard a faint cry. It sounded like someone calling, "Nicky!"

Nicky heard it too. "There's Sally!" he said. "Want Sally!" He got up and the boat rocked alarmingly.

"Sit still!" Jen yelled.

Nicky sat down suddenly. Her tone of voice alarmed him more than the rocking of the boat. Suddenly he was very frightened.

Jen could see Sally racing round the house. Her cry came across the water, even more desperate. "Nicky! Nicky!"

That's one thing done, Jen thought coldly. She can't find Nicky. She's lost the challenge.

Nicky whimpered quietly, shivering and turning purple with cold.

Jen shipped the oars and reached forward to pick up the cormorant. It flopped limp in her hands as she stood up carefully and stepped out on to the rocks. The boat wobbled and bobbed as she took her weight away. Nicky gasped and gripped the sides.

"Jen," he said nervously. "Jen, don't go away!"

"I'm not going away. I'm just going to put the bird down."

"Put it down here!"

She put it down, but only to secure the rope round a sticking-out rock. Then she picked it up again.

"I'll only be a couple of minutes. Stay in the boat and don't move!"

The rocky islet had been swept clean by wind and waves for millions of years. There was no place on it to bury anything. But on the farther edge Jen found a cavity between two rocks and here she placed the bird, anchoring it with a couple of loose stones. The ebbing tide sucked and whispered around her. At high tide the bird would be covered, and it in turn would be swept clean by wind and water, its bones picked by the tiny creatures of the sea.

So that's done too, she thought as she stood up again. Now what?

Give me the child, the voice sighed in her mind.

She turned obediently and went back to the boat.

Nicky was still huddled in the stern. He looked up at her, his face open and defenceless.

Jen held out her hand. "Come here!"

He shook his head. "Want to go home now," he said firmly. Then he added in a very small voice, "Nicky didn't cry!"

He's a brave kid, she thought, unwillingly. It's not his fault the bird died. None of it's his fault.

She listened. The voice was not satisfied. It demanded, *Give me the child!*

But was it really a voice? Or was it just a fantasy inside her own head?

"Come on, Jen," Nicky pleaded.

She shook her head fiercely. The voice gave one last desperate croak.

The child! Give me the child!

The croak was loud behind her. She turned round with a start of fear.

A cormorant was fishing from the rocks. It rose with a fish in its mouth. She saw the ripple in its throat as it swallowed. Then it flew to the rock and croaked again.

One bird was dead. Another lived. A fish died. A bird was fed. The cycle of life and death went round and round.

The light was brightening. The eastern sky was fiery. In the clear dawn light she saw things as they were, cleansed of imagining and superstition. The bird was only a bird, no more, no less, a precious living creature, but not a supernatural being. It had no more power over her. She was sad that a bird had died; she committed herself to protecting life wherever possible, but she was no longer possessed by a cruel and vindictive image of her own making.

Sudden warmth touched her face as she turned towards the land. The sun was rising behind Ardilla. Against the brightness she could no longer see the worn old building. Ardilla was magic, alive with light.

She turned to Nicky, and saw him clearly too. He was just a little boy, very cold at the moment and quite frightened, trying hard to be brave. What was she doing out here with him? She began to shake as she realised what she had done. Had she really brought him out to the island, and into such danger? How could she have done it? What on earth had she been thinking of? Her parents would be furious!

She said, making an effort to sound cheerful and calm, "Come on, mate. Time for breakfast!"

Nicky was shivering violently, but he managed a smile for her. "Long way back, Jen!"

"Don't worry," she replied. "I've done it hundreds of times."

But, as she struggled with a boat that seemed amazingly heavy and oars that seemed to have no pull in them, she realised she had never done it at this particular time of day, when the tide was ebbing strongly and the wind was blowing offshore.

After a few minutes Nicky said, more puzzled than

120

alarmed, "Not getting closer!"

Jen took a quick look over her shoulder. They were about half way between the island and the beach, but they had drifted across the bay until they were almost parallel with the end of the island. In a few more moments they would be out of its shelter. She could see the race of the tide past the rocks at the end and the heavier swell in the open sea beyond.

She pulled harder on the oars, pulled frantically for ten or twenty strokes, turning the bow of the little boat round, until she managed to get back alongside the island. The ebb past the boat lessened slightly, giving her a breathing space. She was not really frightened yet, but she was thinking very fast. She glanced over her right shoulder at the shore, remembering how she had swum that distance earlier. Perhaps she could pull the boat after her more easily than she could row.

Nicky said, his voice rising a bit, "I want to go back, Jen! Let's go back, please!"

"We're going back," she said through gritted teeth. "Just a few more minutes!"

She pulled on the oars hard, trying to get into a long, slow, even rhythm, but when she looked again at the shore, her stomach plunged and she tasted bile at the back of her throat. She was hardly even holding the boat in position. They were no closer to the beach.

The oars were no use to her. They were too heavy and she was too clumsy with them. She shipped them, saying very rapidly as she did so, "Nicky, I'm going to get over the side and try to pull the boat in. You just stay there and sit tight!"

"Nicky row?" he said eagerly. He lifted one of the oars, making the boat rock.

"No!" she yelled. "Just sit still!"

He sat back, hurt, but still trying to be brave.

Jen slipped over the edge. She went under at once. The water was way over her head, and when she surfaced the boat was already drifting away from her. She swam after it and seized the rope, which was trailing in the water. Holding it in one hand, she turned on her side and struck out for the beach. Like a reluctant animal the boat came slowly after her.

If she had felt tired and heavy swimming back to shore with the cormorant, she felt now as if she was made of stone. Several times she thought she would never make it, she would have to give up and let go, but when she raised her head to look at the beach she could see it was getting very slowly closer.

Nicky sat silently in the stern, shivering and gripping on to the sides. Occasionally a larger wave rocked the boat and splashed over the edge. The sun was bright in Jen's eyes and she could see only the outline of the shore, but Nicky saw something that made him wave excitedly.

"There's Sally," he cried. "Sally! Sally! We're out here, in the boat!"

Then he picked up one of the oars and tried to put it in the water.

"Look, Sally!" he yelled. "Nicky rowing!"

A sudden wave rocked the boat, making him pitch forward. The oar slipped out of his hands. It struck Jen hard on the head before it disappeared under the keel.

Jen just had time to see Nicky slip over the side and into the water before her grip on the rope slackened and her stroke faltered. The light and the water seemed to merge. She heard a cry that she thought was Sally's. She realised she needed help and opened her mouth to cry back, but the water rushed in, fierce and salty, and silenced her.

12

Jen was standing on the veranda at Ardilla. It was very early morning. The sun turned the crests of the waves to shining white. Down on the beach she could see Sally plunging frantically through the water. The boat bobbed in the shallows. Nicky was holding on to the rope and trying to pull it up on the beach. He was still wearing his lifejacket.

Good, Jen thought. He's safe. I can go now.

The idea frightened her for a moment, for where was it she had to go?

Then the music started, the consoling, familiar notes of the Bach Partita. Of course, she thought, I must follow the music.

She walked into the house and saw the steps leading down to the cellar. The sound of the music echoed up from below, clear and perfect.

Jen went quickly and lightly down the steps, feeling the cold stone beneath her bare feet. Nothing crunched: the bones and shells had been swept away. The narrow doorway was not guarded. The bird had disappeared. There was nothing to prevent her from going through. Still, she hesitated: the passage beyond was so dark and shadowy. The music called her insistently. She could not turn round. She had to go forward, through the darkness.

At the end of the passage she could see a glimmer of light. Feeling her way with her fingers brushing the rough walls, she went towards it. Because it was dark she was afraid of tripping or stumbling, but it was as if she floated over the paving stones. The light brightened and she emerged into a room, one of the beautiful, unknown yet familiar rooms of the other Ardilla, the one that lay below the surface of the house she knew.

It lay below—yet it was filled with light. She wondered at this, yet it did not really surprise her. Nothing here could surprise her. No matter how new and astonishing everything appeared, she knew that it was how it had to be—and how she had always known it was. Everything was both amazingly new and deeply familiar.

She was happy. Tense, moody, difficult Jen. She saw all those sides of herself and accepted them. She liked them in herself. She would love them into bearing fruit. The tension would become creativity, the moodiness sensitivity, the difficultness originality.

The music was in the room. The player was in the room. Light streamed in so that Jen could not see the figure clearly, but she stood stock still and listened with her whole being, marvelling at the skill and emotion of the playing, wishing that she could achieve it. The Partita came to an end. Another piece began. She recognised the Poulenc flute sonata. She had never attempted to play it herself, but this musician played it perfectly.

She stepped forward.

For a moment she thought she was looking in a mirror.

The musician was herself.

At one with the music, stormy face smoothed out and beautiful.

At the heart of the other Ardilla, the one who could

125

play perfect music was she, Jen.

She spoke her own name aloud, and as she spoke, she heard an echo, as though someone was calling her.

"Jen!"

She shook her head. She didn't want to hear. She didn't want to go back.

"Jen!" The voice was insistent at first and then relentless. Jen stepped forward to her other self, holding out her hand. She would take the flute and she would play like that, and then she could stay here, in the other Ardilla, forever.

Someone was screaming at her. Alternately screaming at her and then trying to suffocate her. Pushing air out of her. No, shoving air into her so she could not breathe. She tried to move, but could not, as in the worst of dreams. Was she awake or asleep? She could not remember.

She thought groggily that she was dreaming. She was having a nightmare. She struggled to wake up, but she could not come out of the dream.

She knew then that she was not asleep. She was awake, but she was dying.

"Jen!" The voice rose to a scream in her ears, and then the scream was all around her, inside and out, hurting her, tearing at her throat, hurting and hurting, with a pain unlike anything she had ever known. The pain took root in her chest, and she coughed and retched to try and get it out.

Then she was vomiting on the beach, sand in her face and hair, on her tongue, in her throat, vomiting the fierce salty water, and moaning with pain and fear.

"Jen." The voice came again, quieter, and scared. Jen turned her head and saw the bright morning sky and, silhouetted against it, Sally's face. Sally's eyes were red with tears and her mouth was bruised and sandy. She was pale and shivering.

"I thought . . ." she stammered, and then gulped.

Jen sat up. She tried to say, "Where's Nicky?", but her voice was no more than a croak and her throat hurt terribly.

"Nicky's all right," Sally said, speaking very slowly and clearly. "I told him to run up to the house and get Dad . . ." Her voice trailed away. "Are you OK?"

"I think so," Jen whispered.

"I had to leave you for such a long time," Sally said, the words coming out in a rush. "I had to leave you in the water while I got Nicky out. I had to choose. I had to get Nicky first. And then I thought you were . . . I thought I'd made the wrong choice."

"It's OK," Jen said. "I'm OK."

Sally gulped again, and then began to sob. The sobs came from deep in her chest, each one racking her slight body. She made very little noise, but the tears rushed from her eyes as though a tap had suddenly been turned on. She shook with sobbing.

"It's all right," Jen said, putting out a hand. She did not know how to comfort people, least of all Sally.

I nearly died, she was thinking, and the shock of the realisation made her tremble all over. I nearly drowned. And Sally saved me.

"Sally," she said, "don't cry! Sally, don't cry!"

But Sally cried on and on. "I don't want to go home!" Finally the words burst out in between sobs. "You've got no idea what it's like! Mum's working and she's always tired, she's always mad at me. I have to look after Nicky the whole time—and I don't mind, I really love him, he's

127

the cutest little kid. And he loves me, he loves me more than anyone does, but sometimes I'd like to get some time to myself. I'm only thirteen! I don't want to be someone's mother already. And I miss Dad so much. I didn't want to come here. I wanted us to go somewhere just us. I knew it wouldn't work out. And it hasn't!"

"We're not going till next week," Jen said. "There's still time—"

"I'm going!"

"You don't have to," Jen said awkwardly.

"Don't kid me," Sally said, starting to sound more angry than sad. "I know you want me to go!"

"I don't any more," Jen said. "I think you should stay!"

"Why?" Sally said with a sneer.

"Well, you tell such great ghost stories for a start." Jen tried to smile but her face wouldn't obey her. She looked away.

Something moved at the water's edge. A little crab ran from a clump of seaweed. It stopped to look around with its stalky eyes and then ran on, leaving a tiny track in the sand behind it.

It was a crab. Nothing more. It was not a symbol or a totem. She saw it with clear eyes. She saw all things clearly, as they were, with no hidden meanings attached to them.

Sally shook her hair, took a soggy tissue from her shorts pocket and tried to blow her nose. "God, I'm freezing," she said. "Come on, we'd better get back to the house. Are you OK to walk?"

Jen was shivering violently, but she struggled to her feet and hobbled up the beach. Crossing the paddock, she stumbled, and Sally caught her by the arm.

"Here, you'd better lean on me."

"Thanks. And listen . . . Sally . . . thanks for pulling me out."

"I was coming down to kill you," Sally said furiously. "How could you have been such an idiot? Nicky could have been—" She broke off and grabbed at the tissue. "Geez, I'm going to start crying again. Dammit, what a disaster!"

They were still some distance from the house when the kitchen door flew open. Mr Fraser came out, still in his pyjamas, a towelling robe over his shoulders. Moving faster than Jen had ever seen him move before, he sprinted to the paddock wall and cleared it in a bound.

Sally stopped short. "I wish I hadn't told Nicky to fetch him," she muttered. "Now he'll start raving again. Here comes another lecture! We'd better come up with a good story."

"Aren't you going to tell him what really happened?" Jen said. I'll have to tell Mum and Dad, she thought miserably. They're going to be so angry. And they'll be right to be angry. I nearly drowned. And Nicky and I might have been swept out to sea and then we both would have drowned. She simply could not stop shivering.

"There's no need to tell the whole story," Sally said. "They'll only go ape, and not let us go out on our own any more. Much better not to worry them."

Mr Fraser slowed down when he saw them. He blinked a bit in the bright sunshine, as if he had woken up too fast.

"I see two very wet girls," he observed as they approached, "who both look as though they've been crying. And I've just seen another very wet kid babbling about birds drowning, and girls falling in the water. But everyone seems to be alive and on their feet." He looked closely at his daughter. "Care to tell me what happened?"

The screen door slammed again and Nicky came running out, dressed in a tracksuit.

"I'm all dry now, Daddy!" he shouted as he climbed the wall.

"More than I can say for you two," Mr Fraser said. "You look frozen. One of you had better wear this." He took off his robe, hesitated for a moment between them, and then held it out to Jen. "Put this on, love," he said. "You look marginally more frozen than Sally." He wrapped it around her shoulders.

"Sally pulled me out of the water," Jen started to explain. "She saved my life." It seemed very important that Mr Fraser should know this.

"That's a bit dramatic," Sally said, off-hand. "She just got out of her depth and got a touch of cramp."

She could have dobbed me in, Jen thought. She could have really got me into trouble. The tears started to well up in her eyes and she shivered and shivered.

Mr Fraser helped her over the wall, then clambered over himself. He groaned and clutched his head. "Fancy waking me up like that," he said to Nicky. "You nearly gave me a heart attack. I'd only just got off to sleep too!" He looked around at the brilliant early morning scene and shuddered. "That sunlight should be banned. It's frying my eyeballs."

Jen looked around too. She saw the old house clearly in the shimmering light. She saw the cracks in the stonework and the peeling paint, and then for a moment her eyes blurred and she saw again the magic Ardilla, the perfect place that would always be part of her childhood.

"Cup of tea all round," Mr Fraser said. "That's what I recommend. Stop your ladyship shivering."

Jen turned her gaze on him, and saw him clearly too, so clearly it hurt. It was as if she had X-ray vision. She saw all his faults, all the things that infuriated her, but she saw his good side too. Suddenly—perhaps it was because she was wrapped up in his bathrobe—she had a flash of how it felt to be him.

He met her eyes and made a funny face at her that seemed to say all sorts of things: that he understood more than he was going to let on, and that he knew she had seen through him. Then he winked at her.

And in that moment it dawned on her that she didn't have to worry about him. She didn't have to worry about all the confusions. She hadn't got rid of them—oh, they would always be there, she was certain of that—but they didn't matter, because she had been to the heart of Ardilla, and she had nearly died getting there, and in that secret, magic place, she had found herself.

She smiled painfully back at him. "If I'm her ladyship," she said, "that makes you my servant, and you have to do what I say. The bird drowned because it swallowed a hook and line. Don't ever let that happen again." She nearly winked back at him, but couldn't quite bring herself to do it.

Sally laughed. "That's telling you, Dad!"

"I tremble and obey!" Mr Fraser said, bowing with a flourish. "Go and get some dry clothes on, while I get the kettle going."

Nicky took Sally's hand and then Jen's. As they entered the old building, swinging him between them, it seemed to stretch and purr in the morning sun. The wind chimes tinkled, and Jen caught the echo of a chant.

At Ardilla at Ardilla at Ardilla.

Also by Gillian Rubinstein

ANSWERS TO BRUT

Kel didn't plan to steal Caspian's bull terrier, Brut, only to borrow him for the weekend. But then Kel's father unexpectedly arrives home and Brut disappears.

Caspian's attempts to find his dog lead him into a dangerous world inhabited by men whom even his parents are too frightened to face.

A powerful story which raises questions about the nature of fear and intimidation and the possibility of confronting them without resorting to violence.

BEYOND THE LABYRINTH

'Weird is my middle name, didn't you know? Brenton Weird Trethewan.'

Brenton finds less and less in common with his family and withdraws into a world of his own pre-occupations where he is happy to let the fall of the dice determine his actions.

Living by the rules of his game gives Brenton a sense of power and purpose missing from his real life. When Victoria comes to stay the dice dictate that Brenton will like her but what draws them together is not chance. The arrival of Cal, an alien anthropologist, brings problems and questions which awaken a new purpose and determination in Brenton's life.

Winner of the Australian Children's Book of the Year 1989

'Rubinstein gives us not one outsider but three, and their perspectives mesh to form a comprehensive critique of our society.' *Melbourne Herald*

'. . . voices the concern that many young people feel about the world they will inherit.'
Australian Bookseller and Publisher

'A terrific book . . .'
Mark Macleod – *The Australian*

SPACE DEMONS

Space Demons is a computer game with a difference. Imported directly from Japan, it's a prototype destined to lock four unlikely individuals into deadly combat with the sinister forces of its intelligence.

And, as the game draws them into its powerful ambit, Andrew Hayford, Elaine Taylor, Ben Challis and Mario Ferrone are also forced to confront the darker sides of their own natures.

'A wonderful book . . . there's so much to enjoy and reflect on.' *Books for Keeps*

'The story is compelling . . . and makes ingenious use of science fiction to create a story of human emotions.' *Horn Book*

Honour Award Australian Book of the Year
Peace Award for Children's Literature
Winner 1988 South Australian Festival Awards

The thrilling sequel to *Space Demons*, *Skymaze*, is also available from Mammoth.

A Selected List of Fiction from Mammoth

While every effort is made to keep prices low, it is sometimes necessary to increase prices at short notice. Mandarin Paperbacks reserves the right to show new retail prices on covers which may differ from those previously advertised in the text or elsewhere.

The prices shown below were correct at the time of going to press.

☐	7497 0978 2	**Trial of Anna Cotman**	Vivien Alcock	£2.50
☐	7497 0712 7	**Under the Enchanter**	Nina Beachcroft	£2.50
☐	7497 0106 4	**Rescuing Gloria**	Gillian Cross	£2.50
☐	7497 0035 1	**The Animals of Farthing Wood**	Colin Dann	£3.50
☐	7497 0613 9	**The Cuckoo Plant**	Adam Ford	£3.50
☐	7497 0443 8	**Fast From the Gate**	Michael Hardcastle	£1.99
☐	7497 0136 6	**I Am David**	Anne Holm	£2.99
☐	7497 0295 8	**First Term**	Mary Hooper	£2.99
☐	7497 0033 5	**Lives of Christopher Chant**	Diana Wynne Jones	£2.99
☐	7497 0601 5	**The Revenge of Samuel Stokes**	Penelope Lively	£2.99
☐	7497 0344 X	**The Haunting**	Margaret Mahy	£2.99
☐	7497 0537 X	**Why The Whales Came**	Michael Morpurgo	£2.99
☐	7497 0831 X	**The Snow Spider**	Jenny Nimmo	£2.99
☐	7497 0992 8	**My Friend Flicka**	Mary O'Hara	£2.99
☐	7497 0525 6	**The Message**	Judith O'Neill	£2.99
☐	7497 0410 1	**Space Demons**	Gillian Rubinstein	£2.50
☐	7497 0151 X	**The Flawed Glass**	Ian Strachan	£2.99

All these books are available at your bookshop or newsagent, or can be ordered direct from the publisher. Just tick the titles you want and fill in the form below.

Mandarin Paperbacks, Cash Sales Department, PO Box 11, Falmouth, Cornwall TR10 9EN.

Please send cheque or postal order, no currency, for purchase price quoted and allow the following for postage and packing:

UK including BFPO — £1.00 for the first book, 50p for the second and 30p for each additional book ordered to a maximum charge of £3.00.

Overseas including Eire — £2 for the first book, £1.00 for the second and 50p for each additional book thereafter.

NAME (Block letters) ....

ADDRESS ....

....

☐ I enclose my remittance for ....

☐ I wish to pay by Access/Visa Card Number

Expiry Date